To andrea
Happ...

D1353262

# Andrea

# SPRINGSONG ❧ BOOKS

Andrea

Anne

Carrie

Colleen

Cynthia

Gillian

Jenny

Joanna

Kara

Kathy

Lisa

Melissa

Michelle

Paige

Sherri

SPRINGSONG  BOOKS

# Andrea

## Gloria Chisholm

BETHANY HOUSE PUBLISHERS
MINNEAPOLIS, MINNESOTA 55438

*Andrea*
Gloria Chisholm

Library of Congress Catalog Card Number 83–71614

ISBN 1–55661–622–8

SpringSong edition published 1995
Copyright © 1983
Gloria Chisholm

All rights reserved. No part of this publication may be
reproduced, stored in a retrieval system, or transmitted in
any form or by any means electronic, mechanical,
photocopying, recording, or otherwise without the prior
written permission of the publisher and copyright owners.

Published by Bethany House Publishers
A Ministry of Bethany Fellowship, Inc.
11300 Hampshire Avenue South
Minneapolis, Minnesota 55438

Printed in the United States of America

To my son, Travis—
a source of constant encouragement

GLORIA CHISHOLM is a free-lance writer and editor from Seattle, Washington. A single mother of five, she has written seven books and hundreds of articles and short stories for many Christian publications.

# 1

*T*he doors of Brookdale Community Hospital parted automatically. Entering the building, I fought the desire to turn and run.

I hated hospitals. The smell of antiseptic hit me, nearly causing me to gag. I shouldn't have come, but the need to see Neil and to be reassured that he wasn't seriously injured pushed me forward. I soberly followed his younger brother down the narrow corridor.

Curiosity caused me to glance into the occupied rooms we were passing, and each time I wished I hadn't.

My discomfort must have shown, because Grady stopped and turned to face me.

"Are you okay?" he asked.

I nodded. "I'll be all right." *As soon as I get out of here,* I thought to myself. "When do you think we'll be able to see him?"

Grady shrugged. "When he's out of surgery, I guess."

"When's that?" I asked.

"I don't know. A couple more hours, maybe."

*At least two more hours until I see Neil!* I wondered how bad he'd look. Would I be able to hide my shock if he had lots of visible cuts and bruises? He needed my support.

Neil's parents met us at the door of the waiting room.

"Has there been any change?" Grady asked hopefully.

Mr. Hollinger shook his head. "He's still in surgery." He nodded in my direction. "Hi, Andrea."

7

Mrs. Hollinger, a tall, stately woman, didn't even acknowledge my presence.

"We haven't heard anything since you left to pick up Andrea." She nervously twisted the scarf around her thin neck and sat down on one of the plain couches that furnished the small room.

I continued to stand uncomfortably by the door as Grady sat down beside his mother. He motioned to the chair across from him.

"I wish they'd at least come and tell us something—anything." Mrs. Hollinger leaned forward, anxiously looking out into the hall.

"Go ahead and sit down, Andrea," Grady said.

I walked past Mrs. Hollinger to the chair Grady had pointed to and sat down stiffly.

"I don't suppose Neil was wearing his helmet?" I ventured, afraid of the answer.

"Does he ever?" Mr. Hollinger answered from his position at the door.

"Were you with Neil last night?" Mrs. Hollinger finally spoke to me.

I nodded.

"Then I suppose he was coming home from your house this morning when he had the accident?" Her eyes narrowed.

"He left about one o'clock," I told her.

Was this a hospital or a courthouse? What was she trying to do, blame me for Neil's accident?

"It happened about two-thirty." Her tone was one of suspicion.

I avoided her piercing stare. Why was I letting her get to me?

"Did Grady tell you about it?" Mr. Hollinger's soft voice rescued me.

I shook my head.

"Neil ran a red light, and a van hit his motorcycle broadside. The driver of the van has only a few cuts on his head."

Neil and I had watched the late movie the night before. Now that I thought about it, it was probably after two o'clock when Neil left. It seemed an irrelevant detail, and I didn't figure it was worth mentioning.

"Had he been drinking?" asked Mrs. Hollinger.

"No." We had smoked a little pot, but I didn't want to mention that. It was bad enough that the accident was Neil's fault, and I didn't want to get him into any more trouble.

I knew I should have stayed home. I didn't belong here with Neil's family and I really didn't want to deal with all of this questioning. Although I appreciated Grady for thinking of me, I'm sure the Hollingers hadn't suggested that he bring me here.

Mr. Hollinger ran a hand through his graying hair and stared solemnly at Grady. "You're praying, aren't you, son? It looks bad, and God is our only hope."

Grady nodded firmly, but I noticed his lower lip slightly trembling.

"He's right, Grady." Mrs. Hollinger tried unsuccessfully to smooth a wrinkle in her skirt. "We need to pray like we've never prayed before. I dedicated Neil to God when he was a baby and his life is in the Lord's hands."

It wasn't that serious, was it? Oh, why didn't they shut up? They weren't helping any. It was so like them to bring up religion—and make everyone feel worse.

It was because of their religion that I'd never hit it off with the Hollingers in the first place. Neil had mentioned on more than one occasion that his parents didn't approve of me because I'd dragged him away from church. It wasn't true. Although he had gone fairly regularly with his parents until we met, he'd lost interest in church long before we started dating.

I'd met Neil at a party at the beginning of the previous

summer. I'd had my eyes on him all through high school, but then so had most of the other girls I knew. I never did figure out why Neil chose me, but I don't think either of us was quite prepared for the sudden emotional intensity of our relationship. Who has time for church when you're in love? I reasoned. In spite of the disapproval of Neil's parents, our mutual feelings for each other made us inseparable all summer long.

The Hollingers weren't easily discouraged in their attempts to keep us apart, though. They were forever trying to match Neil up with nice little church girls who were the daughters of their friends. In their eyes I'd never be good enough for their angel.

He was an angel. Neil's handsome face came clearly into focus now. Of course all I had to do was look at Grady. Although Grady was two years younger, they could have been twins. Both had dark brown wavy hair, but Neil's was a little longer than Grady's. They had the same laughing brown eyes, which were definitely inherited from Mr. Hollinger. They both had a medium build, but Neil was a little more muscular.

The only thing Grady needed was the blue cap that lived on Neil's head. He rarely took it off.

Why couldn't he have worn his helmet last night? Sometimes he did, but he felt that a helmet inhibited him when he rode his motorcycle. I agreed. What was the fun of it if your head had to be locked in like that? It defeated the purpose.

Now I began to feel differently. Neil might change his mind about it too when he got out of here. He *would* get out—I was sure of that. It bothered me that everyone looked so glum. Didn't they know that Neil was strong? He wouldn't let this accident get him down.

The swinging doors moved and everyone in the room turned in that direction.

A young doctor strode across the room to two young men standing by the window. I couldn't hear what he said because of a toddler jabbering away and a typewriter clicking ninety miles an hour in the next room. It must have been good news, because a look of relief passed over their faces.

The doctor walked briskly from the room and the two youths hurried past us and out the door.

I glanced around at the other people in the room. A thin, elderly man sat on the couch behind me twisting his ragged handkerchief. The mother of the toddler followed her child around the room trying to keep him out of trouble. On another couch sat a husband who was trying to console his wife, but her tears wouldn't stop.

What a creepy place. Poor Neil! The sooner he got out of here, the better.

I tried to imagine Neil lying on a hospital bed, but couldn't do it. He was too alive in my mind. I could still hear his parting words last night:

*"I love you, Andrea," he whispered as he pulled my thin figure near to him and closed his leather jacket around my shoulders. The smell of the leather awoke in me once again a certain kind of toughness about Neil that I'd always admired.*

*"I love you too." I reached up and wrapped my arms around his neck. "I've missed you so much."*

*"Thanks for waiting for me. It's going to be a great summer."*

*Then he kissed me hard, sending me into a dream world. I didn't come down to earth until I heard the roar of his bike as he sped away from my house.*

"Do you want a cup of coffee?" Grady broke into my thoughts.

"Coffee? No thanks," I answered. What I craved was a cigarette, but I'd never before smoked in front of the Hollingers. I couldn't see any reason to make this situation any more uncomfortable than it already was.

"What time did you get to the hospital?" I asked.

"About three-thirty," Grady answered.

I glanced at my watch. "You mean he's been in surgery for six hours? Why so long? How badly was he hurt? Have you told me everything you know, Grady?"

Grady glanced sharply at his parents, as if searching for a clue as to how much I needed to know.

Mrs. Hollinger shuddered. "He looked awful."

"You mean . . . you saw him after the accident?" I asked.

"We were here when the ambulance arrived." Mr. Hollinger's eyes refused to meet mine. "I'm afraid his condition is serious."

I looked from one to the other of Neil's family, searching their faces for more clues. Neil wouldn't die. He wouldn't leave me. He had told me that many times. He was the first good thing that had happened in my life. We hadn't actually discussed it, but I was sure we'd get married someday even though a year of high school still loomed ahead of me.

This past year had been difficult for both of us. We saw each other only once or twice a month on weekends. He'd been home from college only a week. This accident would interfere with our future plans. How long would he have to stay in the hospital? Suddenly I thought about his bike. Neil worshiped that motorcycle. He used every spare moment to work on it.

"Is his bike totaled?" I asked no one in particular.

Mrs. Hollinger shot me a look of disgust.

"Yeah," answered Grady. "I went and looked at it. It's a mess."

"That's too bad," I mumbled. "Neil worked so hard to get it the way he wanted it."

"Buying that motorcycle was the worst thing he ever did!" Mrs. Hollinger's face flushed as she screeched the words at me. "I never wanted him to buy it. I worried every time he rode it. He wouldn't be in that operating room right now if he would have listened—"

"Marilyn." Mr. Hollinger spoke firmly. "It's no use thinking like that. With Neil hanging between life and death, we need to keep thinking positively."

If it wasn't religion, it was positive thinking. If Neil were here, he would reassure them that he was going to make it, that there was nothing to worry about. Neil seldom worried. He thought it was a waste of time and energy.

I hated this waiting. I'd be glad when this whole thing was over and I could once again be with Neil, see him smile, feel his arms around me. At the first possible moment, he'd walk right out of this hospital. He didn't like to be cooped up.

Once again the doors swung open. As the middle-aged doctor stepped over to Mr. Hollinger, we all jumped up from our chairs to join them.

"We did everything we could." He paused and looked thoughtful, as if choosing carefully his next words. "His brain was hemorrhaging badly. We tried to stop the bleeding, but it was already too late when they brought him in. He died a few minutes ago. I'm very sorry."

# 2

*N*o! It was impossible! The doctor must have mistaken us for someone else. He couldn't be talking about Neil.

Mrs. Hollinger's face turned white as she gasped for air and grabbed her husband's arm.

"Your son was strong." The doctor eyed them sympathetically. "He held on longer than is normal for this type of brain injury." He lowered his eyes. "Uh, why don't you folks sit down? I'll change and be back in a few minutes."

As he turned to leave the room, I suddenly felt as though I was going to be sick. I sank down into a chair and caught my breath. Had that doctor really said that Neil was dead? My Neil?

It couldn't be. We were supposed to go to the beach tomorrow with some friends. Not Neil—I just wouldn't believe it, that's all. That doctor was crazy, just like everyone else. I had to get out of here.

I got up to leave, but someone grabbed my arm. I turned and saw—Neil! Of course not—it wasn't Neil, it was Grady.

"Where are you going?"

"I don't know—away from here."

"You can't—I mean, let me take you home." He looked so tired, ready to collapse, yet his grip on my arm remained strong.

Mr. Hollinger lowered himself onto the couch and dropped his head into his hands. "Dear God, dear God . . ." he repeated over and over while Mrs. Hollinger clung to him and softly sobbed.

*I should be crying too.* Why wasn't I crying? It was because this whole episode wasn't really happening. I would go home and wait for Neil to call today like he'd promised he would. When he called, he'd tell me the whole thing was a horrible case of mistaken identity. That was it, of course; they had him confused with someone else.

Grady had released his grip and was seated next to his mother, gently patting her shoulder with one hand while studying me closely.

*Neil, where are you?* my heart cried. *Please shake me. Help me wake up from this awful nightmare!*

"Let me take you home," Grady repeated.

I nodded.

He turned to his parents, but I didn't wait to hear what he said to them. I half walked, half ran through the hospital corridors and outside into the brightness of the day. How could the sun shine when Neil lay dead in that cold building behind me. Dead? No—hurt, maybe. I think I could handle that. Seriously injured—we'd make it because we had each other. But dead—no, please, not dead! He couldn't be dead.

I searched the parking lot for the gray Chevy. I ran in and out between cars in the general vicinity of where we'd parked. When I finally located it, I climbed inside, grateful that Grady hadn't locked the doors.

I sighed with relief. I was safe in this car. No one could hurt me now—not that doctor with his cruel words, nor Neil's parents with their unjust accusations.

This car was so much a part of our life together. Sitting here, I could sense Neil's presence, hear his laugh, feel his touch. The Chevy belonged to him originally, but when he'd left for college, he had sold it to Grady. He rode his motorcycle the two hundred miles back and forth to school and borrowed the Chevy from Grady on his weekends home. We'd shared so many good times in here. Memories, both sad and painful, began to roll through my mind.

I jumped when the car door opened. Grady settled himself behind the wheel and stared at me for a minute.

"Are you going to be okay?" he finally asked.

"No, are you?" I shot back.

"I don't know—I might be if I could somehow understand God's—"

"God!" I screamed, cutting him off. "God! Where is your God, anyway? Was He sleeping when Neil was killed? Face up to reality. If there is a God, He doesn't care about you, me, or anyone else. If He did, He would have saved Neil's life."

My words, like a sharp knife, sliced the air between us into a thousand pieces.

A pained expression crossed Grady's face, but he didn't answer. He started the car, and we drove in silence.

I didn't feel like talking. I just wanted to be in Neil's car, to memorize every detail, because this was probably the last time I would ever ride in it. I touched the blue dashboard, took mental note of the two speakers in the back window that had blared out our favorite songs, and fingered the small brass hook under the dashboard where Neil hung his cap on hot days.

A wooden cross now hung from the rearview mirror. Grady and his religion. I wondered how long it would last now that Neil was dead. Certainly he would realize now that my opinion about God was true, and that was why he couldn't find an answer.

"I don't have an answer for you," Grady began as we pulled up in front of my house, "but that doesn't mean there isn't one."

"I don't want an answer," I blurted out. "I want Neil." The sobs suddenly tore from my throat and I finally cried. "Oh, Grady, I'm sorry—you must feel as awful as I do."

I was so caught up in my own pain, I had overlooked his.

He sighed. "I don't know why he died. . . ."

I tried to focus my eyes on Grady, but everything blurred together.

Suddenly I just wanted to be alone. I opened the door and climbed out of the car. "Thanks for the ride."

Grady turned his head slowly in my direction, but I didn't know if he really saw me. "Sure," he said.

I slammed the door and stumbled into the house, hurrying past my mother who was talking on the phone.

I ran to my room, threw myself on the bed, and began to cry bitter tears. I beat my pillow and screamed at a God I didn't believe in. When I exhausted my supply of hateful things to say to God, I buried my head in my pillow and moaned.

Suddenly my mother's shrill laugh pierced my consciousness.

"Isn't that the funniest thing you've ever heard? And then Chuck mentioned something about her new hair color and it started all over again. Hey, I'll have to call you back. Andrea's throwing a fit in her bedroom, and I should probably try to find out what's going on. I'll talk to you later. Bye, now."

In a moment, my mother appeared at my bedroom door. "What in the world are you so upset about?" she asked.

I sat up in bed and leaned back against the wall. "Neil was in an accident last night," I told her. "He's dead."

"Oh no, Andrea!" Mom put her hand to her cheek in shock. "That's awful! He was so young. . . ." She sat down on the edge of my bed. "How did it happen?"

I wasn't ready to talk about it.

"I'll tell you later." I pulled my knees up to my chest and rested my chin on them. "I don't feel like talking about it right now."

She got up quickly. "Of course. Well, whenever you feel like talking, just let me know. I'll be here."

*Oh, sure,* I thought, as she patted my arm, *if something more important doesn't come up in the meantime.* I watched my mother's small figure disappear around the corner and then I lay back down. My eyes refused to stay open and I drifted off into a deep sleep.

When I awoke three hours later, my body ached. I struggled to remember what had happened to make me feel so rotten.

I sat upright in bed when the stark reality of Neil's death hit me again. *Was this whole thing a bad dream from which I was now awaking?*

The recent hours at the hospital were still too fresh in my mind. *If I could just erase this day of my life—if Neil had only left my house five minutes earlier or later—if . . .* It was too late to think that way. Neil was gone.

I couldn't imagine life without Neil. It would be unbearable. I lived for the times when we could be together. When we were apart, I thought about him constantly.

No, I couldn't live without Neil, but the alternative frightened me more. I feared the future without him, but I feared death even more. What was death, anyway? Where was Neil now? Could God possibly exist? Did life have a purpose? If God wasn't real, I'd sure wasted a lot of energy screaming at no one.

Yet something inside assured me that my screams and cries hadn't bounced off the bedroom walls. For the first time in my life, I became aware of Someone who knew my thoughts completely and who also knew where Neil was at this moment. I didn't know whether I liked that or not. I felt something between a feeling of relief and fear of the unknown. I tried to remember everything I'd learned about God in Sunday school. I used to go every Sunday on the church bus with the neighbor kids. It was such a long time ago, and I could hardly remember anything I had learned.

I hadn't been to church since that time except for a couple of weddings.

I jumped when my mother poked her head into my room. I'd scared myself with all those thoughts about death and God. I was glad to see something familiar again, even if it was only my mother's curly blond head.

"Would you like some dinner?" she asked.

I suddenly realized I was a little hungry. I hadn't eaten since yesterday, so I stretched my legs and got up. I followed her down the hall and into the dining room, where I was relieved to find the table set only for the two of us. My mother invited her boyfriends for dinner far too often lately.

I stirred the peas around on my plate and tried to relay the details of the accident to my mother without getting tears all over my food. Every time I tried to talk, my emotions rose up and the words caught in my throat.

The phone rang and I jumped up to answer it. Then I solemnly sat back down, realizing that it wouldn't be Neil.

Seeing that I wasn't going to move again, Mom leaned over to pick up the receiver.

"Hello? Yes, just a minute."

I took the receiver from her. "Hello?"

"Hi, Andrea. This is Grady."

He sounded exactly like Neil on the phone. Maybe if I closed my eyes and concentrated real hard . . .

"Are you there?" he asked.

"I'm sorry, Grady. I'm here."

"How are you?"

"Fine," I lied.

"You don't expect me to believe that, do you? You can be honest with me."

Could I really? Could I tell him that Neil was my reason for waking up in the morning? Would he understand that every smile that crossed my face was for Neil? He had no way of knowing that my once happy thoughts now tormented and taunted me, robbing me of my purpose for life.

I'd never been able to share my feelings easily, and I wasn't about to start with Grady, whom I hardly knew.

"I'll be okay." I tried to sound convincing.

"The memorial service is going to be Tuesday at ten o'clock." His voice sounded hoarse. "I just thought you'd want to know."

"I'll be there. Thanks for calling, Grady."

As I hung up the phone, I looked at my mother.

"I guess he feels responsible for me, or something."

"That's nice of him."

"I suppose." Suddenly, pain from deep inside became almost unbearable. "How am I going to make it, Mom? I don't even want to live."

The doorbell rang and my mother gasped. "Oh, dear. That must be Chuck, and I'm not ready."

I groaned inwardly as she ran out of the dining room to let him in.

Chuck! Something or someone always interfered with any closeness I struggled to have with my mother. At that moment I wished I could have thrown myself into her arms and cried like those times when I was a little girl and had skinned my knee. We didn't share that kind of relationship anymore. Ever since my dad's death when I was eight years old, my mother and I had gradually grown apart. Now we hardly knew each other.

She had dated a number of men since then, Chuck being the most recent.

I could now hear them in the living room, talking quietly. She then came back into the dining room, eyeing me uncertainly for a moment.

"Would you like to go to a movie with us?" she asked finally. "It would help take your mind off Neil."

I didn't want to take my mind off Neil.

"No, thanks. You go ahead. I'll be all right."

"Oh, c'mon," she persisted. "We can't leave you in this state of mind."

"Hey, I don't need to be baby-sat," I returned. "I just don't feel like going to a movie, that's all."

"Andrea . . . if you don't go, we can't either. We've decided—"

The phone rang, abruptly ending the explanation. Out of habit, I impulsively reached for it.

"Andrea . . ." It was my best friend, Terri. "I heard about Neil. You must feel—just horrible. It's so hard to believe, isn't it?" She paused, and then in a rush of words said, "Look, we just talked to Drew and he's still having his party tonight. Rich and I want to come by for you."

I'd forgotten about Drew Bradshaw's party. Not that I would even consider going without Neil.

"Thanks, Terri, but I don't really feel like going out tonight."

"We'll talk about it when we get there. We'll be right over."

Before I could protest, she'd hung up. I faced my mother.

"You can go now. Rich and Terri are coming over."

"But they might not stay long. I don't want you here alone tonight."

"Your mother's right," Chuck agreed. "If your friends leave early, we'll be at the Broadway. Call us and we'll come home."

Chuck was a nice guy. He went out of his way to be friendly to me. He was a handsome man with dark, curly hair and a bushy moustache. He hung like another bead on my mother's necklace. I was sure he wouldn't be the last.

I nodded. "Sure, Chuck."

Chuck stared at me for a moment. "I'm awful sorry about Neil. I guess there's really nothing I can say to make you feel any better." He put his arm around me. "Just know that I'm hurting for you, and if you ever want to talk about it, I'll listen."

"Thanks." I bit my lip to keep from crying. I wished they'd leave, but Chuck took his time helping my mother with her coat and then couldn't find his keys.

The doorbell rang as he found them in an inside pocket of his jacket.

"Now don't forget to call us if they leave," Mom called over her shoulder as they went out the door, greeting Rich and Terri on their way.

Terri stepped into the room ahead of Rich and our eyes met. She pulled at some strands of dark hair, as if doing so might cause her new short haircut to grow again. We'd always worn our hair alike since our friendship began in third grade. By getting her hair cut, Terri had wanted to show her individuality and desire to be her own person. Although it kind of hurt me, at seventeen, I suppose we were old enough to start doing different things on our own.

As we faced each other now, I realized how grateful I was that they had come.

Terri took a breath. "Since I've known you, this is the first time that I can't quite think of what I want to say to you." She hesitated. "And anything I try to say will probably come out wrong anyway."

"You don't have to say anything. I'm just glad you're here."

As we hugged, our tears flowed together. It felt good to finally be able to share them with someone. Rich stood close-by, and I noticed the pain in his eyes as he silently joined us in our grief.

When we had finally gained some sense of control, Terri said, "We all know the party tonight won't be the same without Neil, but don't you think he'd want us to be together tonight, Saturday night, same as always?"

"I suppose," I admitted. "But what's the point? I'd just

sit in a corner and cry all night."

"We'll be right there with you. Right, Rich?"

Rich nodded. "Drew said to be sure to bring you. Look, Andrea, we're all hurting, and that's all the more reason why we should be together."

"Oh, okay." I opened the hall closet and grabbed my sweater. Then I wrote my mother a note, telling her not to expect me until late. Drew's parties never broke up until two or three in the morning. Even at that late hour, the refrigerator remained full of beer.

That was it. If I could get enough to drink, I could forget this terrible nightmare for a while. That's what I would do—get good and drunk.

# 3

$\mathcal{I}$ awoke on Sunday morning, my head threatening to blow like the lid of my mom's old coffee maker. From the smell that floated into my bedroom, I quickly concluded that the coffee was already perking away on the stove.

I sat up slowly and rubbed a hand across my pounding forehead. At least these hangovers never lasted long. I knew I'd feel better as soon as I got up and moved around a bit. *But what should I get up for? There was nothing to do, nothing to look forward to.*

I'd spent most of the previous evening drinking beer, crying, and talking to Drew Bradshaw about Neil. It was apparent that everyone was upset about his death, almost to the point of being morbid. As the party progressed and the beer began to disappear, much of the grief seemed to turn to anger. When two guys got into a fight on Drew's front lawn, we decided to leave.

In the distance I heard the phone ringing.

"Andrea, are you awake?" my mother yelled from the dining room.

I clamped my hands over my ears. Why didn't she come to see if I was awake instead of yelling like that?

"Who is it?" I yelled back.

"I don't know. Some guy."

I dragged myself out of bed and glanced quickly into the mirror. My eyes were bloodshot and puffy from crying, and my mop of brown curly hair was matted to my head. What difference did it make? I wouldn't be seeing anyone.

"Hello?" I mumbled into the phone.

"You sound like I feel," Drew remarked.

"Don't let my voice fool you," I quipped. "I sound good compared to the way I feel."

Drew chuckled. "Did you decide if you're going to the beach with us?"

"The beach?"

"Yeah. Don't you remember? I didn't want to be the fifth wheel today. You said you'd think about it and let me know when I called."

"I did?" Actually, I remembered very little of what happened after about nine o'clock the previous evening.

"No, I guess you don't remember," Drew went on. "Well, that's understandable. So think about it now. It'll help take your mind off Neil."

Another ploy to take my mind off Neil.

"No, thanks," I answered dully. "I have plans."

It was true. I needed to take a shower and wash my hair.

"What are they?" Drew wanted to know.

I should have known he'd ask. He was that kind of person.

"I . . . uh . . . have to do some things around the house." I cradled the phone on my shoulder as I began clattering the pots and pans together and throwing them into the dishwasher. "The house is a mess and my mother expects me to help her clean it."

I didn't want to go to the beach with him or anyone else. How could they just go on with their plans like this—like nothing had changed—as if Neil hadn't died?

"You've got all summer to clean the house," Drew persisted.

"I really don't feel good either." I tried to sound sick.

"Okay, okay." He finally conceded. "But you're going to miss a good time."

*No way,* I thought. *There is no such thing as a good time without Neil Hollinger around to keep things moving.* They would find this out for themselves soon enough.

"Thanks anyway, Drew."

I hung up the phone and began to methodically rinse the dirty dishes in the sink and put them into the dishwasher.

When I accidentally broke a glass, I watched the blood cover my thumb and drip down into the sink. I felt no pain. What was pain, anyway? I'd lost Neil.

Sunday dragged by slowly. Monday was just as bad. My thoughts revolved around Neil and nothing else. I didn't *want* to think about anything else.

Torrents of tears came and went. Whenever I was sure I had cried the last tear, a certain memory of Neil would shoot through my mind and I would burst into tears all over again. Would it ever end, this whole feeling of frustration, helplessness, and inability to cope?

The day of the memorial service dawned bright and sunny. As I gazed out the window at the clear blue sky and listened to the chirping of the robins, the day seemed to suggest a new beginning. But with Neil's memorial service to face, this day was just the beginning of the end.

The walls of the plain white church building were already bulging when my mother and I entered. At least five hundred people had crammed themselves into the sanctuary. Extra chairs were brought in and were quickly filled. Latecomers stood along the side walls and also at the rear of the church. It was apparent that Neil had touched a lot of lives.

The pastor, a young man in his early thirties, said many nice things about Neil. I could have told that audience so much more. I could have told them about the gentleness in his eyes when he said, "I love you"; the tenderness of his kiss; the firmness of his hands massaging my back at the end of a tiring day. These remained my own special memories to be tucked away in my heart forever.

The service itself lasted only forty-five minutes, and then people began streaming out of the church and onto the lawn outside. Neil's parents stood on the steps greeting people. Grady stood beside them, talking to some kids from school. As we passed him, he grabbed my arm.

"We're having an open house today," he said. "Can you come?"

I glanced at Mrs. Hollinger.

"Yes, Andrea, do come over." She nodded politely. "And bring your mother."

"Thank you, but I have plans for today," my mother apologized. "I'm sure Andrea will be there, though, won't you?"

I found it hard to believe how much Grady looked and acted like Neil. I watched him, fascinated, as he extended his hand to an older couple whom he seemed to know well. After offering their sympathy, they went on their way. Grady, turning back to me, met my staring eyes. A slow grin spread over his face. He reminded me so much of Neil, and the fresh memory sent a sharp pain through my stomach.

"Andrea?"

"Huh? Oh, sure, I'll be there."

My mother patted Mrs. Hollinger's arm. "I'm sorry about Neil," she said. "I admire your courage to stand here smiling and talking when I'm sure you don't feel like it."

"Oh, it's not me," Mrs. Hollinger returned quickly. "It's the Lord. He gives me His strength, you know."

"Of course." But my mother looked confused, then turned to me. "Ready?"

I nodded, and we headed for our car.

"Oh, it's not me!" I imitated Mrs. Hollinger, throwing my shoulders back. "It sure looked like her, didn't it?"

"You could have fooled me," Mom agreed. "But she said it was the Lord."

We both laughed.

"I wonder why they're having a private burial," I muttered as we drove out of the parking lot. "It's not fair to the rest of us."

"They're awfully religious," she answered. "Maybe they want to pray or something without a bunch of onlookers."

"Yeah." I slumped down in the seat and stared out the window. "Do you think Neil's in heaven, Mom?"

She thought for a moment. "I've never really believed in heaven or hell, but if they're real, I'm sure Neil went to the right one. He was a fine young man. I'm surprised at how well you've handled his death."

I smiled wryly but didn't answer. She didn't know how much I was hurting inside, and I wasn't about to tell her. She had seen me cry only that first day. She'd been busy with Chuck and too preoccupied with her secretarial job to notice my hurt. She probably figured now that the memorial service was over I'd forget about Neil and go on with my life as though he'd never existed. That was not going to happen.

I wondered how she had felt when my dad died. All I remembered before his death was their constant arguing. She couldn't have grieved too much.

As I freshened my makeup, I began to feel a little apprehensive about going alone to the Hollingers. Most of the crowd would probably be family, friends, and relatives. Neil avoided family gatherings as much as possible, so I hadn't met many of his relatives. I didn't think any of our crowd would be there. Grady's friends would probably go. Although we'd both be seniors this fall, I'd always considered Grady's crowd so much younger. It wasn't because they acted that way, it was probably because I was accustomed to Neil and his friends. Everyone else seemed dull and immature by comparison.

I dialed Terri's number and was relieved when she answered the phone. I thought Rich might have taken her out after the service.

"Grady invited me to his house today for a . . . reception or . . . I don't know what you call it," I began. "Would you go with me?"

"I thought you'd be going to the burial," Terri said.

"It's private."

"Private? You were as close to Neil as any of his family . . . probably even closer."

"You know Neil's mother. I wouldn't have even been at the hospital when he died if it hadn't been for Grady."

"Poor Grady," Terri sympathized. "I wonder if he has to go through what Neil went through when it comes to dating."

"I don't think Grady poses the same problem as Neil did. I'm sure he dates only *nice* girls."

"Yeah, he's into their religion trip too," Terri agreed. "Nancy's here. We were going to come over to see you anyway."

"I'll pick you up in a few minutes," I said.

A few minutes later, they climbed into my car. So did the heavy scent of Nancy's favorite perfume. She always poured on half the bottle. I often wondered how her boyfriend, Bruce, could stand it.

"What is this thing we're going to?" Nancy pulled a strand of her long blond hair out of her face.

"I don't know what they call it," I answered. "I guess it's similar to the reception after a wedding."

"Weird," Nancy remarked. "You'd think everyone would go home and cry instead of celebrate. Do you think there will be any cute guys there?"

Nancy had a one-track mind.

"I don't know who's going to be there," I said. "Probably some of Grady's friends, but they're all a bunch of religious freaks. Maybe some of Neil's college friends—"

"Super." Nancy's face lit up. "It's rare that I get to go anywhere without Bruce."

Nancy had been dating Bruce for a few months, but stayed alert in case a better offer came along.

"Nancy, I think the Hollingers are having this so everyone can pay their last respects to Neil," Terri interjected.

"I'm aware of that." Nancy waved a hand at Terri. "But you never know what might happen. I like to be prepared."

Six cars were already parked in the Hollingers' circular driveway, and both sides of the street were full when we arrived.

"It seems strange coming here today without Neil around." Nancy voiced what we were all thinking.

"This is where I met Bruce for the first time. Of course, I'd seen him around school, but never thought I'd get a chance to meet him. But he told me he thought I was the prettiest . . ."

Nancy's voice droned on as we opened the gate to the Hollingers' estate. I looked for a familiar face among the cluster of kids sitting on the lawn. I recognized two of them, but didn't know them well enough to approach.

Grady met us at the door, holding it open as we stepped inside.

"I'm glad you came," he said.

"Do you know Terri and Nancy?" I asked.

"Just from school. It's good to see you. Make yourself at home. I have some things to do, but I'll get back to you." He pointed to the dining room table. "Help yourself."

We made our way through the throng of people to the table with various types of hors d'oeuvres and desserts.

"What a layout!" Terri exclaimed as she slapped several different types of cheese on her plate. On the chunky side, she complained about her weight occasionally, but never seemed to do anything about it.

In contrast, Nancy didn't even take a plate. She

munched on a carrot as she scanned the room, probably looking for a handsome face. Suddenly a look of disgust spread across her face as she saw Bruce heading toward us.

"I thought you weren't coming," Nancy accused.

"I changed my mind." Bruce grabbed a plate and began piling it up. "I don't trust you out of my sight."

"Oh, Bruce, don't be ridiculous." Nancy laughed. "Do you think I'm interested in anyone but you?"

"Sometimes it's questionable," he muttered.

Bruce hadn't bothered to dress up. It was obvious that he had come on his motorcycle, because his hair was windblown and his jeans were spotted with mud.

Terri and I began milling among the people, talking to those we knew. Eventually we ran into Grady standing among his friends. He was holding hands with the redhead beside him.

"Hi again," Grady greeted, then introduced us to the group around him. His girlfriend's name was Cheryl Riley.

"Do you go to Sunset High too?" Cheryl smiled sweetly. We nodded.

"We just moved to California a few months ago," Cheryl went on. "The kids at Sunset are so friendly."

"It's a friendly school," Terri said. "We've got a great football team. I suppose Grady has already told you that."

"He's mentioned it." Cheryl looked adoringly at Grady. "I can't wait to see him play."

Grady blushed.

"It was nice meeting you." I pulled at Terri's arm. "I see Drew over there."

Drew's blond hair was sun-bleached and his skin a shade darker, probably from the beach trip. His deep blue eyes lit up as I approached him. Turning from his buddies, he draped his arm lightly over my shoulders.

"Hey, how's it goin'?" he asked. "I thought maybe I said something at my party to hurt your feelings since you wouldn't go to the beach with us."

"No, it wasn't anything like that," I reassured him. "It's just that, well, I'm afraid I wouldn't have been much fun to have along."

Drew would understand. He and Neil had been roommates and close friends at college. Drew had graduated from Sunset High in Neil's class, but I hadn't officially met him until I began dating Neil. I still didn't know him very well, but he seemed nice.

He nodded. "That's okay. It'll take time for you to get over Neil. It's not easy for me either, and I just thought . . . since we have mutual needs . . . that we could, uh, kind of help each other through this. You know what I mean?"

What he was saying was that we needed each other. I admired his honesty.

"I'll think about that," I told him.

"Why do you always have to think about things?" he asked. "Don't you know how you feel?"

Of course I knew how I felt. I needed Neil, and no one else would ever be able to satisfy my need. And although a lot of people loved Neil, no one loved him like I did. So no one, not even Drew, could understand how I felt.

"This isn't exactly the place to talk about it, is it?" I returned.

He misunderstood and turned to me eagerly. "Your place or mine?"

"Quit pressuring me," I hissed.

He stepped back. "I'm sorry. I just want to help. I guess I'm trying too hard." He put out his hand. "Friends?"

I took his hand. "Friends." I turned to Terri, who was fidgeting nearby. "Ready to go?"

"Yeah. Rich is coming for dinner."

"I suppose I should talk to Neil's mom before I go."

"What for?"

I shrugged. "It's just something my mother taught me, I guess."

I scanned the faces in the room and found her near the kitchen. When I reached her, she was deep in conversation with another well-dressed woman. She finally noticed me and stopped talking.

"I don't want to interrupt," I said, aware that this was exactly what I was doing. "I just want to thank you for inviting me. I had a nice time."

"Well, that's good." Mrs. Hollinger placed a hand on the lady's arm beside her. "Andrea, this is Ruth Riley. They recently moved here from Idaho." She turned to Mrs. Riley. "Andrea was an acquaintance of Neil's."

*An acquaintance? Who is she kidding?* She made me furious.

I returned to Terri. "Mrs. Hollinger is so complimentary." I scowled. "Where's Nancy?"

"She's going home with Bruce."

We started out the door, but stopped when we heard someone calling my name. I turned to see Grady coming toward me.

"Can I talk to you for a minute?" he asked, then glanced at Terri.

"I'll wait in the car," Terri said as she headed down the steps.

"I'm sorry we didn't get to talk more," he began. "I wanted to ask you . . . there's going to be a good band at the Paramount this Saturday night. They're called Dayspring. Would you like to go?"

Grady's laughing brown eyes were just like Neil's. They had a way of making a person feel completely at ease.

I hesitated.

Grady picked up on it. "Hey, if you'd rather not . . . I just thought . . . well, they're a good group and . . ." He looked uncomfortable.

I didn't have any plans for Saturday night. Now that Neil was gone, I didn't have any plans, period. My life was suddenly a big nothing, a void.

"I'd like to go," I found myself saying.

Grady looked pleased. "I'll pick you up at seven."

I walked down the concrete steps deep in thought. Grady wasn't Neil, but he was the next best thing.

# 4

*I* drove to the cemetery Wednesday morning to take Neil a bouquet of yellow roses I'd picked in our yard. After asking where his grave was, it took me only a few moments to find it—*Neil Anthony Hollinger*. Seeing his full name engraved on a tombstone made it all seem so—so final. He wouldn't come back to me, not ever.

Forever stretched out before me—mile after mile of endless time. Each mile took Neil farther away from me. My heart hit my stomach with a sickening impact when I brokenly calculated the distance between us.

*Why couldn't I have been on his bike with him? We would be together now.*

Flowers of all varieties and colors covered Neil's grave. Mine paled in comparison. But then, if from his vantage point he could look down and see me on this hillside, he would possibly appreciate mine the most.

I knelt down on the ground and lifted my head to search the clear blue sky for an answer. What did I expect? A message written in the clouds? Nothing came.

Neil had truly loved me. No one who touched my life now really cared whether I lived or died. My mother loved me in her own shallow way, but it was obvious that her main concern was Chuck. Terri had been a loyal friend for a long time, but her love for Rich now consumed her. I couldn't think of anyone who would be terribly upset if I died tomorrow. Was taking my life an option I should seriously consider?

I was such a coward. I almost passed out when Terri and I pricked our fingers with a pin in fourth grade, vowing to be blood sisters forever.

If it involved pain or blood, I wouldn't be able to kill myself. With my luck, I'd botch it and be paralyzed for life.

I frowned at Neil's tombstone.

"How could you do this to me, Neil?" I cried aloud. "You promised you'd never leave me. You promised. . . ."

Sobbing, I ran to my car and climbed in.

How long would it be until I wouldn't cry every day for Neil? Would the thought of him haunt me forever?

———————

Terri and I went shopping on Saturday so I could buy a new pair of jeans for my date with Grady.

"Grady's different than Neil," Terri said as we ate lunch at the local diner just outside of Sunset. "What do you have in common?"

I shrugged. "Neil?"

"I'm not sure that's enough."

"It's only a date, Terri. If we talked about Neil the whole night, it would be okay with me. There's nothing I'd rather talk about."

"That's fine for you." Terri chewed on her fingernail thoughtfully. "But it might not be what Grady has in mind. What's the name of that band?"

"Dayspring."

Terri frowned. "I've never heard of them. Are they new?"

"Grady said they're supposed to be good. That's all I know."

"You'd better watch it," Terri warned. "Knowing Grady, they'll probably begin their concert with 'Amazing Grace' and end with 'Jesus Loves Me.' "

I couldn't help laughing. Terri and I thought alike. I

could tolerate the lyrics if the group had good musicians.

That evening my mother appeared at the bedroom door and watched as I dressed for my date.

"Where are you going?" she asked.

"Out with Grady Hollinger."

"Neil's brother?" She looked surprised. "When did he ask you? You didn't tell me."

I sighed. "Yes, I did."

I'd mentioned it at least twice. She never listened.

"He's so much like Neil, you won't believe it." I turned to face her. "He—"

"Huh—how about that. . . ."

She was gone.

Our conversations were like that—little snatches of dialogue thrown into each other's lives, caught, then discarded quickly. I didn't know why I even bothered.

The doorbell rang as I was brushing my hair.

"I'll get it," I yelled and ran to the front door. I stopped a few feet away. It might be Chuck. He was due anytime now too. Grady might have even changed his mind about tonight. I'd probably get a call any minute.

I threw open the door and almost cried aloud with relief. There stood Grady looking almost as handsome as Neil. He really did want to take me out or he wouldn't be here.

"Hi." That slow grin spread across his face as he stepped inside.

"Hi." I enjoyed just watching him move. His mannerisms reminded me so much of Neil.

My mother entered the room, breaking the spell.

"I'm not sure we've formally met each other." Grady warmly received her outstretched hand.

I introduced them, and at the same time started toward the door.

"I'm so sorry about your brother," she sympathized while glancing at her watch. "I wonder where Chuck is. Are things returning to normal at your house?"

What a dumb question—as if anything could ever be normal again with Neil gone.

Grady shrugged. "I guess so."

"Your mother seems to be holding up well," Mom continued.

"She's doing okay."

*At least she hasn't committed suicide* was what I picked up from his tone of voice. Mom was too insensitive to notice.

"I'm surprised at Andrea. She's going right on like—"

"We'd better go," I interrupted. This small talk with Mom was killing me.

"It was nice to meet you," Grady said politely as we moved out the door. "I'll have Andrea home by twelve o'clock."

"Oh? Well, don't worry about the time. I trust Andrea."

I knew she'd rather I didn't bother coming home at all. I was only an inconvenience when Chuck was around.

Grady opened the car door and I slid onto the familiar blue upholstery. This car even smelled like Neil. It was probably a combination of marijuana and his favorite brand of cologne. I didn't want to be in here with anyone other than Neil. I hoped my face wouldn't betray my feelings. As long as Grady didn't try to touch me, I'd survive. I hugged the door.

As we pulled away from the curb, I struggled to think of a topic of conversation that might interest Grady. All I could think of was religion, but I didn't want to get into that. I wanted to ask him some questions about Neil, but this didn't seem quite the right time. Maybe I could ask him a question about his car. . . .

I chanced a sidelong glance at Grady. I wondered if he was as nervous as I was.

"You'll like Dayspring." Grady finally broke the awkward silence after we'd driven a few blocks.

"Dayspring," I repeated. "That's a different name for a band."

"It comes from a verse in Luke. 'The Dayspring from on high has visited us,' meaning Jesus Christ, of course."

Of course. Who else? Terri was right. Dayspring was a religious group, and this promised to be a boring evening unless, of course, the music was as great as Grady claimed.

We had to park five blocks away from the Paramount. The warmth of the day's sun lingered on, and I didn't mind walking. Grady stayed by my side. He was different from his brother in that regard. I'd always had to half run to keep up with Neil's long strides.

I'd been to many rock concerts at the Paramount, but this crowd was different. Missing was the restless, wild undercurrent of a bomb about to explode. I still felt the excitement and anticipation that's always present before a band performs, but the crowd was relaxed, unlike any I'd ever seen at the rock concerts I had attended.

Many of the kids knew Grady. Before we found our seats, he'd introduced me to at least fifteen people. Everyone greeted one another as if it had been years since they'd been together. The strangest feeling came over me. I felt as though I'd entered a huge room full of family members, but for some reason I felt excluded, like a foster child entering a well-established family might feel.

A group called David's Band came on stage. I settled down expecting to hear melancholy church hymns, but was I ever surprised. I'd anticipated maybe an organ and a couple of harps. Instead, I watched the group tune up their electric guitars and arrange their drum set. Maybe this wouldn't be so bad after all.

It wasn't. The words sounded somewhat religious, but surprisingly enough their music exploded into the auditorium and held my attention. Still, how anyone could get excited about God and heaven was more than I could grasp.

As Grady had promised, the other group, Dayspring, was excellent. The acoustic guitar player caught my attention right away. I noticed it because Neil had always had a secret desire to learn to play the guitar. He had loved jazz.

When they announced an intermission, Grady turned to me, "What do you think?"

"I love them!" I said enthusiastically.

He grinned. "I knew you would. I'll go get us something to eat."

I wondered why Grady had asked me to this concert, and I wondered where Cheryl Riley was tonight. The fact that it was none of my business didn't stop me from speculating. Maybe Cheryl had left town for the weekend. Could they have broken up?

I wasn't sure of Grady's motives for asking me out. The important thing was that he *had*, and I didn't want him to be sorry. I determined to perk up and try my best to make some intelligent conversation on the way home.

I didn't have to work this hard to make conversation with Neil. We didn't even find it necessary to talk much of the time. We just loved being together. The memory of his hand touching my cheek was enough to send me into a fantasy world during those times he was away at school. Oftentimes I wouldn't return to reality until he came back to visit.

I suppose the comfortable kind of relationship Neil and I shared didn't happen overnight. Yet, I could hardly remember a time when we'd felt awkward with each other.

Grady returned and handed me a Coke and a bag of popcorn. He casually dropped a Dayspring CD into my lap. I looked it over and began to return it to him. He put up a hand to stop me.

"Keep it," he said. "I already have one."

"Grady, thank you! That was sweet of you."

This was the kind of thing Neil would have done.

"I'm glad you like the group," Grady said in between mouthfuls of popcorn. "I think Neil would have liked them. I tried to get him to go last time they were here."

"He wouldn't?"

"He had a date."

"With me?"

Grady shrugged. "I never kept track."

I stared at Grady. Were there that many?

He caught me staring at him and grinned sheepishly. "That was a dumb thing for me to say, huh? Anyway, it was probably before he met you."

Even so, I hadn't realized there had been so many girls in Neil's life. He had only mentioned a couple of former girlfriends.

I clapped as hard as everyone else did when Dayspring returned to the stage. They slowed their music down for the second half of the concert. Involuntarily I stopped being so wrapped up in the group's instrumentation and found myself concentrating on the words of the songs. They made God sound so—well—so personal, through the person of Jesus Christ. Could it be possible that God actually spent His valuable time thinking about me, Andrea Marie Lyons?

I wasn't sure I liked that. God probably held high expectations for my life, and how could I possibly live up to them?

To be honest, I rarely thought about God until Neil died. God might have loved me at one point, but did He still love me now even though my life had become so empty? I had excluded God from my life, and now my very best friend, the center of my life, was dead. I had no desire to live, so lately I resorted either to smoking pot or drinking beer until I passed out or at least until I could forget the misery I felt inside. Sometimes I lay on my bed and fantasized about my times with Neil. I wondered how long I could keep running.

*If God really cared, why didn't He do something?*

"What else can God do?" the lead singer challenged as the group concluded their final song. "He gave His Son who gave His life for you. The Bible says if we draw near to God, He'll draw near to us. It's your move now."

*My move? What was I supposed to do?* I glanced at Grady. He must miss Neil, yet his relationship with God seemed to remain intact. I wondered if he too shared my need to escape. Did knowing God somehow compensate for that?

Suddenly I experienced an urge to stand and scream, "Okay! I can see that you've got something. I want it. So how can I get it?"

"You can know the Jesus we've been singing about," he continued. The instruments became quiet and a hush settled over the audience. "He loves you and wants to give you the joy and peace you've been searching for."

*Okay. How?* I waited for the snag.

"All you have to do is ask Him."

*It can't be that easy!* I cried inside. *Peace can't come that easy.*

"Confess to Jesus that you're a sinner," he went on. "Ask Him to forgive you and to come into your life. He can do a much better job of controlling it than you can."

I had no doubt that God could control my life better than I could. I knew I was living wrong and had long ago stopped caring or counting the cost of my selfish behavior. But could He forgive my past? take away my guilt? give me peace? Anyway, what did I have to lose?

"You don't have anything to lose," the speaker was saying. "And everything to gain."

He then instructed those of us who desired to know Jesus on a personal basis to go ahead and pray. A few moments of silence followed, which would have been very uncomfortable if I had stubbornly chosen not to respond, but I did respond. I prayed earnestly and sincerely.

At last I knew in my heart that God understood the

depth of my pain in losing Neil, that He loved me, had forgiven me, and that He even wanted to do something about this awful loneliness I felt inside. Hope sparked from somewhere deep inside of me. It was like a flicker of light at the end of a long, dark tunnel.

Grady hesitantly slipped his arm around my shoulders, and I buried my head in his chest, letting the tears soak into his shirt.

I clearly understood now the family atmosphere in this room, and I no longer felt like a foster child.

As we left the auditorium that evening, raindrops danced lightly on the pavement, but nothing could dampen my frame of mind. We walked quickly to the car and climbed in. Then we turned to each other and smiled as if we shared together a wonderful secret.

As we started driving home, silence pervaded, almost as though whoever spoke first would be breaking a magic spell.

Suddenly, as though a firebomb had exploded into a quiet green meadow, an unanswered question penetrated my mind.

"Neil didn't share your family's faith in God," I began. "Grady—where do you think he is now?"

Expecting to hear the worst, I held my breath while waiting for his answer.

"Neil believed in the Lord." Grady seemed to be choosing his words carefully. "I walked beside his stretcher all the way to the operating room. I told him Jesus loved him a lot and that all he needed to do was to pray and ask Jesus to forgive him."

I sighed with relief. "He would have prayed, I know it."

"Right before I had to leave him, he nodded like he understood what I was saying. I believe he's in heaven, Andrea. I only wish he'd had a chance to live for God." He reached out to touch my hand. "We'll see him again someday, you know. You made an eternal decision tonight."

"Is that the reason you brought me?" I couldn't help asking. "So I would make that decision?"

He grinned sheepishly. "Are you accusing me of ulterior motives?" His expression turned serious. "With Neil gone, I knew that you didn't have purpose in your life anymore. A long time ago Jesus gave purpose to my life that even Neil's death couldn't shake. It would be selfish of me not to share it with you."

We arrived home far too soon. I wanted this evening to last forever. Chuck's station wagon sat parked in its usual spot in the driveway. There was no hope of even a short chat with my mom now.

"Would you like to come to my church tomorrow?" Grady asked as he turned off the engine.

"Okay," I agreed.

"It starts at eleven," he faltered. "I wish I could pick you up, but my parents need me to be with them now."

"I understand."

He took my hands in his and gazed into my eyes. "What you did tonight will affect your whole future. Christianity isn't a onetime experience. It's a lifestyle. Do you understand?"

I wasn't sure I did, but I nodded anyway.

"We'll talk more about it later."

I wanted desperately to prolong this evening.

"You'll come in, won't you?" I asked as we walked up the drive.

Grady shook his head. "It's too late. Maybe some other time."

Neil always stayed for an hour or so after our dates.

Grady squeezed my hand. "See you," he called over his shoulder as he got into the car.

I rattled my key in the lock and slammed the front door behind me. Chuck and my mother sat curled up on the couch in front of the television. Assuming they were asleep, I tiptoed past them.

"You're home early," Mom mumbled.

It was twelve-thirty. Neil and I normally stayed out until at least one-thirty or two o'clock.

"Grady has to get up early for church, I'll bet," she slurred and laughed loudly.

An empty liquor bottle balanced precariously on the edge of the coffee table. Throwing her a disgusted look, I retreated to my room. I undressed and crawled into bed. Suddenly I remembered that I should pray first. I got up and awkwardly knelt by my bed, trying to think of the proper way to address God. I couldn't think of anything profound to say, so I simply thanked God for Grady and told Him that I would be so grateful if Grady would ask me out a second time.

I still missed Neil more than ever, but being with Grady tonight had somehow helped alleviate my incredible sense of loss. At times, Grady emanated the personality of Neil to such a degree that I indulged myself in imagining that nothing at all had happened to Neil. I followed a simple routine. When Grady laughed, I heard Neil. When Grady stressed a point and wrinkled up his nose, I saw Neil. When Grady touched me, I felt Neil's touch. I'd been able to forget for a short while that I'd lost the person who meant everything to me.

I needed Grady. I wanted to see him again; but now that I'd become a Christian, Grady might consider his mission accomplished and stop pursuing a relationship.

What about Cheryl Riley? How much of Grady's time did she demand? Would she understand that Grady and I needed each other?

I felt an uneasy awareness that my dealings with her in the future would be less than pleasant.

# 5

The shrill ring of the alarm clock woke me. It was ten o'clock. I reached over and clicked it off, trying to remember why I had set it.

Oh, yeah—church. Did I really want to get out of my cozy, warm bed to go sit in a stuffy building with a bunch of strangers?

I yawned, stretched, and wiggled my toes. It felt good to wake up with a clear head. In the past, many Sunday mornings had started out with a horrendous headache and a sick stomach.

On a rating of one to ten, how strong was my desire to go to church? No more than a five, I calculated.

Then a positive thought occurred to me. I'd get to see Grady. I must have been half asleep not to have considered him. The rating quickly shot up to seven.

The phone rang and I impulsively jumped up, remembering Neil. Then reality threw me into despair. I'd never again hear his voice on the other end of the line.

I waited to see if my mother would answer it. When it continued to ring, I forced myself out of bed. Maybe it meant someone was thinking about me—it could be Grady.

"Hi, Andrea," Nancy's high-pitched voice greeted me. "It's going to be eighty-five degrees today. Let's go swimming at the river."

"Swimming?" I stalled as I struggled to think up a good excuse. I certainly couldn't tell her what my plans were for today. She'd laugh herself sick. "I . . . uh—I'm going to be pretty busy this morning. Could I meet you there later?"

"What do you have to do?" Nancy persisted.

Knowing Nancy, she wouldn't be satisfied until she knew every last detail. *This isn't fair,* I thought angrily. *If I had known she was going to call, I would have had a nice speech prepared telling her about the changes taking place in my life. Now I've allowed her to put me on the defensive.*

*Lie to her,* an inner voice prodded. *Tell her something— anything.* For some unexplainable reason, I couldn't even think of a good lie.

"What do you have to do?" Nancy repeated impatiently.

"I . . . uh . . . I promised Grady I'd meet him some-where," I finally blurted out.

"Grady Hollinger?" Nancy laughed. "It couldn't be much of a secret rendezvous if he's involved! I hear you went out with him last night. You're wasting your time. What in the world do you talk about to a religious freak? They all have one-track minds." She paused. "Hey, this is Sunday. You're not going to church, are you?"

"Well . . . yes, I am," I muttered. I hated myself for not being more bold.

Nancy groaned. "I can't believe it. One date with Grady and you're sucked in already. Listen, Andrea, you don't want to sit in a hot church on a day like this."

"But I promised Grady—"

"So what?" Nancy interrupted. "He'll go whether you're there or not. Bruce bought us some beer. Maybe we can pick up some guys who have a boat and talk them into taking us waterskiing."

That did sound fun.

"Terri will be here any minute," Nancy went on. "C'mon. The three of us haven't done anything together for a long time."

That was true. Besides, Grady would be with his parents

at church. Even if we saw each other, we wouldn't be able to talk long, if at all.

"Oh, okay," I agreed, disgusted with myself for giving in. It was really Grady's fault, I reasoned. If he'd offered to pick me up, it wouldn't have been so easy for me to back out.

As I threw my swimsuit on and jumped into a pair of tan shorts, I kept hoping that my mother would wake up. I wanted to tell her about my date with Grady and my experience with God. Not that she would be all that interested, but if living for God was a lifestyle, as Grady had conveyed, then I needed to prepare her for the changes to come.

She hadn't gotten up by the time Nancy and Terri drove up in Nancy's Camaro. The car had been a present for her sixteenth birthday.

I climbed into the backseat and we roared off.

I glanced down at the case of beer beside my feet. Beer had always meant only one thing to me—escape. I despised the taste; I drank only to get drunk.

Funny—I didn't feel like getting drunk today. Something must have really happened to me last night.

"Didn't Bruce and Rich want to come along?" I asked.

"Oh, yeah," Nancy answered. "I promised Bruce I'd be good, but I suppose he'll show up sometime today."

Cars were parked bumper to bumper along Marine Drive. As a result, we had to park over the hill and then trudge all the way back in the burning sand to reach our favorite spot.

We dumped our belongings on the sand and scanned the beach to see if we knew any of the people sitting around on their towels.

Nancy opened a can of beer and began to chug it down.

"Go ahead, we don't even have to pay Bruce for this. It's on him. Isn't that sweet? Every once in a while he does something that assures me I'm smart to hang on to him. Not often, but occasionally."

"I'm . . . I'm not thirsty," I said casually as I passed a can to Terri.

"Who's thirsty?" Nancy laughed. "I just want to get drunk." Her expression turned serious. "C'mon, Andrea, don't ruin the party."

"I just don't feel like drinking." I laid my towel out carefully and sat down, hoping she wouldn't press the issue.

"It's okay, Nancy," Terri put in quickly. "More for us."

Nancy shrugged. "Have it your own way, but if it has to do with religion, I think you're nuts." She put the bottle to her lips again and finished it off.

At least with Nancy, I always knew where I stood. Of the many feeble thoughts that tossed themselves around in her mind, I could be sure that most or all of them would be expressed through her mouth.

"Speaking of religion." Nancy winked at Terri. "Tell us about your hot date last night."

I wasn't sure I could put into words what had happened the previous evening. Should I gloss over it and give them only the highlights or should I express some of the depth of my feelings for God? Terri would at least try to understand, but Nancy would be Nancy. I wasn't sure I could deal with being laughed at. On the other hand, I'd explode if I didn't tell someone. Terri and Nancy were my best friends. Although I couldn't quite explain it myself, somehow I wanted to tell them as much as I could.

I took a deep breath.

"I enjoyed the concert. The band was different than what we're used to; their songs were mostly about God."

"Figures." Nancy lit a cigarette and leered at me. "You weren't expecting Grady to take you to a bar?"

I ignored her. "At the end, the leader told us that we could know Jesus Christ personally." I tried to choose my words carefully. "He asked us to repeat a prayer. So I did. I really feel different inside. I don't hurt so much about Neil."

"What did I tell you?" Nancy poked Terri. "One date with Grady and it's all over."

Terri shrugged. "I think it's okay. If anything ever happened to Rich, I'd want to kill myself. If this can give Andrea the guts to face life without Neil, it can't be so bad."

Nancy sighed and rolled her eyes.

"Well, Nancy, take a look at her," Terri persisted. "She looks a lot better than she did at Drew's party."

"I suppose," Nancy admitted grudgingly. "So you need a crutch for a while. Whatever makes you feel good. I've seen enough religious nuts to know that they always want to push their beliefs on everyone else. Personally, I think it's a little side trip that won't last long, but while it does, don't bug me with it. I'm having too much fun to think about God, life after death, and all that morbid stuff." She opened another beer. "Okay?"

I nodded. "Sure, Nancy, I wouldn't push anything on you."

"Anyway, what we really wanted to know about last night was what happened with you and Grady. Did he kiss you?"

I shook my head. "It wasn't that kind of a date."

Nancy laughed. "What other kind is there?"

"Did he ask you out again?" asked Terri.

"No."

"Look at that, would you?"

We followed Nancy's gaze to a red speedboat roaring by. I silently thanked God for the interruption and hoped our conversation would not continue.

"Bruce told me that Drew wants to ask you out," Nancy said, turning back to me. "But he's not sure how you feel so soon after Neil."

I liked Drew, but the thought of dating him didn't particularly thrill me.

"I'll love Neil as long as I live," I admitted. "I'm not so sure I ever want to love anyone else again. The only reason I went out with Grady is because I was tired of sitting home crying every night."

That wasn't completely true, and I felt disloyal to Grady for saying it. So why had I gone out with Grady? I wasn't sure myself. All I knew was that I had to remain true to Neil. Grady and I were just friends and would most likely stay that way. I felt grateful to Neil because he had left in Grady a part of himself for me to hang on to.

Drew was a different story. He obviously wanted more than a friendship.

As I had hoped, the conversation didn't return to God or my date with Grady. Of course, the more Nancy and Terri drank, the less communicative they became. I could steer our chitchat in just about any direction and they barely noticed. Eventually, as usual, Nancy began flirting. Some of the guys were real creeps. Nancy had almost committed us to an all-night raft party when Bruce showed up. I could have hugged him.

Not only did that mean no more flirting, but it meant that we would be leaving soon, because Nancy tired of Bruce easily.

I was right. Shortly after Bruce arrived, Nancy began gathering her stuff together. She could hardly walk, let alone carry anything. I trailed behind her, picking up whatever she dropped.

We waved goodbye to Bruce and climbed into the Camaro, everyone agreeing that I should drive. Nancy and Terri chattered on about their dates with Bruce and Rich that evening as we drove home. Hearing them talk reminded me of how alone I was.

"Bruce said he can get you a date tonight," Nancy offered.

"No thanks," I returned. Most of Bruce's friends were my friends, and none of them appealed to me in the least.

It would be a lonely evening, but the alternatives looked worse. If I couldn't have Neil, I'd rather be alone.

I arrived home to find my mother in the kitchen frying bacon.

"Hi, Andrea," she greeted. "Would you like a bacon, lettuce, and tomato sandwich?"

I nodded. I was starved.

"Did anyone call?" I asked.

"Just Neil's little brother," she replied. "Greg—or what's his name?"

Grady had called! He'd looked for me at church and missed me. I could have kicked myself for giving in to Nancy's whim.

"His name is Grady. I was supposed to meet him at church this morning. He probably called to find out why I wasn't there."

"Church?" Mom echoed in a surprised tone. "Why would you want to go there?"

I didn't expect much more of a favorable response from my mother than I had received from Nancy and Terri. I decided to tell her because I knew she'd eventually find out anyway.

"Promise you won't laugh," I said.

"I promise."

"I became a Christian at the concert last night."

"Oh?" She looked amused. "And how did you do that?"

"I asked Jesus Christ to forgive my sins and to come into my life."

"Just like that? One, two, three, zap, and you're a Christian?"

"I guess so. I don't understand it all myself. That's why

I want to go to church—to learn more about it."

She sighed. "I suppose Grady talked you into this."

Mom set two plates on the table and placed our sandwiches on them along with a helping of potato salad.

"No, it was my own decision."

"I don't know why you went out with him," she continued. "He's not your type at all."

"That's true, but now that I'm a Christian, we'll have more in common."

"Do you think you'll be seeing him again?"

I shrugged. "We had a great time. At least I did."

"Andrea." She eyed me soberly across the table. "I don't care if you want to go to church, but I've seen people go fanatical over religion. The Hollingers are a good example. If I see you going overboard, I'll put a stop to it. I'm not going to have my daughter turn into a religious nut. Is that clear?"

My mouth dropped open. I'd expected her to be amused, but I hadn't expected this. She had seldom shown any interest in my life. She hadn't cared if I smoked or drank. I had even stayed out overnight with Neil many times. Yet now she was getting uptight about the first right thing I'd done.

"Is that clear?" she repeated.

"It's clear," I muttered. "But what do you mean by fanatical?"

"I mean sitting around with your nose in a Bible, going to church every chance you get, and talking about religion constantly. It happened to your aunt Martha. Eventually she got over it, but she was a nuisance for a long time."

"But, Mom, it's made such a difference inside of me. I feel different. I still miss Neil, but some of the hurt is gone."

"That's nice," she said. "Maybe this is what you need to help you get over him. It probably won't last. I suppose I shouldn't come down so hard on you. It's just that Aunt

Martha became so difficult to live with. It temporarily ruined her."

I pushed my plate away, leaving half a sandwich. Without a word, I got up from the table and went to my room, kicking the door shut behind me.

No one understood. Everyone thought I was crazy. Was I? If so, then Grady and his family were crazy along with all those people at the concert last night. They hadn't looked crazy, only happy—happier than any group of people I'd seen before in my life.

As the vivid memory of asking Jesus into my heart came rushing back, I realized that what I'd done hadn't been crazy at all. Contrary to popular opinion, it *would* last. I would hold on tightly and make sure it did. It was my last shred of hope. I now had a purpose for living.

# 6

$\mathcal{G}$rady had suggested that I start reading the Bible, beginning with the book of John. First I had to *find* a Bible. I was sure I'd seen one somewhere in the basement. Mom would know right where it was, but I wasn't about to ask her.

I searched until I finally found it under a pile of Mom's high school yearbooks. It smelled musty, like it hadn't been opened in twenty years.

I could understand why. It was a huge book! I read through the book of John for an hour and made it through only eight of the twenty-one chapters.

I'd hoped that by reading this book my unanswered questions would be explained. Instead, I found that reading only raised more questions.

I bet Grady had all the answers. He'd been a Christian for a long time. As soon as he called, I would ask him.

Grady didn't call on Monday or Tuesday. I began to think that his interest in me had been intended to last only until he had converted me.

At the center of my every waking moment were thoughts of Neil. When my mind wandered even slightly from Neil, Grady became the focal point. What was he doing? Was he thinking about me at all? Would I ever see him again? Why should I care?

The intensity of missing Neil did not diminish with time as I had hoped it would. Instead, it seemed to control even a larger part of my thoughts.

Wednesday came and went and Grady still had not called. I devoured the book of John and the book of Acts. I had even more questions I needed to find the answers to.

Should I call him? No. The questions I had could make my mind go crazy before I'd let him know how much I needed his friendship.

When he finally called on Thursday, I bombarded him with questions.

"Why do you think Jesus chose Judas to be an apostle when He knew he was going to betray Him?" I began. "Do you have to be born again more than once?" I asked. "You know, in the book of Acts where—"

"Hold it, hold it." Grady laughed. "One at a time, please. You might as well know now, I don't have all the answers."

"You don't?" I couldn't hide my surprise.

"Of course not. The important thing is that you're reading the Bible."

"I thought you'd be able to help me."

"I'll do the best I can," Grady promised. "The reason I called is to see if you'd like to go with me tonight to our youth meeting at church. We cover a lot of territory in the Bible, and I'm sure some of your questions will be dealt with and answered."

Was Grady asking me for another date? "I'd love to. What time should I be ready?"

Before hanging up, he promised he'd come by at seven o'clock to pick me up. Grady hadn't forgotten about me after all. Seven o'clock was only four hours away. Even though I must have been an afterthought, that was better than not being thought of at all.

When I heard a car pull up into the driveway promptly at seven o'clock, I grabbed my leather jacket out of the hall closet and, dropping into the platform rocker by the front door, waited for him to ring the bell.

Mom looked up from her crossword puzzle. "Where are you going?"

"To a youth meeting at Grady's church."

"Sounds exciting. What's a youth meeting?"

The doorbell chimed.

"Beats me," I called over my shoulder. "I'll tell you later."

"It's good to see you again." Grady grasped my hand when we were in the car.

I stiffened involuntarily at his touch. The memory of Neil touching me was still too fresh. He jerked his hand away as if I'd burned him.

"What's the matter?" he asked.

"I miss him so much, Grady." My tone of voice pleaded for sympathy and comfort.

"Yeah, me too."

He hurts too. Why couldn't I see past my hurt to remember that he had lost a brother?

"We started cleaning out his bedroom this week," he went on. "We're going to put it off for a while. It's too hard on my mom."

"I'm sorry, Grady."

"That's one reason I didn't call. I want to be there for you, but it's been a tough week for me in a lot of ways. It's a good thing I was the one who found Neil's hash pipe and cigarette papers. It would kill my mother if she knew Neil took dope."

"It wasn't that big of a deal with him." I found myself defending Neil. "We smoked pot occasionally, but everybody does that."

"He was into heavier stuff," Grady persisted.

"What do you mean? We promised each other we'd never get into anything heavier."

"You don't know what he did at college," Grady countered. "Without being disrespectful to Neil's memory, I'm sure you know that honesty wasn't one of Neil's outstanding virtues. Oh, he never lied purposely, I don't think. He just didn't always 'fess up to all the facts. He had his reasons. Lots of times it was to protect someone he cared about."

"Well, how would you know what he did at college anyway? Neil never lied to me, I know it." I felt myself becoming angry at Grady for even suggesting such a thing.

"I never said Neil lied to you," Grady answered quietly. "He loved you, Andrea. Forget I said anything."

The subject seemed closed as we pulled into the church parking lot, but I meant to bring it up again at the first opportunity. I couldn't believe Neil would take dope behind my back.

The memory of Neil's funeral renewed itself as we entered the church by a side door and descended the stairs to the basement. I soon forgot about it as I followed Grady into a room full of kids my age who were sitting on couches or pillows on the floor. Every eye turned toward us as we entered the room. Maybe Grady had told them about me. What could he have said?

I hated new situations like this. I didn't know anyone in the room. Whenever I had gone with Neil to someplace new, I'd clung to him, letting him do the talking. He never seemed to mind.

This group looked friendly. Grady began to introduce me around the room. In my embarrassment and uneasiness, I forgot everyone's name. He finally led me to a couple sitting on a couch. I sensed they were someone important in his life. I immediately recognized them from school. Among my friends, they were classified as "super-straights."

"Andrea, these are my friends Marc Steele and Jill Wagner."

They smiled warmly as we sat down beside them. *If Terri and Nancy could see me in this room with all of these straights, they'd really think I flipped,* I thought to myself.

"What time is this over?" I asked.

Grady's attention was elsewhere. I followed his gaze to where Cheryl Riley stood in the doorway. Soft red curls framed her face. When she saw Grady, she headed right toward us.

Grady scooted closer to me so she could sit between him and Marc. It was quite cozy when she sat down. Too cozy. I couldn't remember when I'd felt so uncomfortable. I knew it wasn't just the tight seating arrangement that made me so uncomfortable. Who was I in Grady's life anyway?

One of the guys started strumming a guitar, and the group of twenty-five to thirty kids began singing so enthusiastically that I expected the walls to cave in at any minute. It reminded me of going to camp when I was younger.

After the singing ended, the guitar player asked for testimonies. I leaned back in my seat wondering what a testimony was.

One girl told the group about how God had spared her from a car accident. Another guy gave God all the credit for an A in geometry on his final report card. While he was talking, Grady nudged me.

"You have a testimony to share, Andrea," he whispered.

"I do?"

"Sure. Tell them how you met Jesus."

"I don't know them that well."

"Then I'll do it."

Before I could protest, Grady gained the attention of the crowd, introducing me as Neil's girlfriend and recounting how I had become a Christian at the Dayspring concert. I stared at the huge cable rug, memorizing every fiber and not daring to look up to meet anyone's eyes. When he had finished, I shyly lifted my head and was surprised to see genuine smiles of friendship on their faces. They accepted me openly without my having to prove myself.

Whenever I wanted to be associated with a certain group

at school, I always had to earn their approval first. Even Nancy admitted to me once that she thought I was straight and stayed away from me until she saw me at an all-night party with Neil. Then she knew I was "okay."

Actually, I *was* straight until I met Neil. Then suddenly I was thrust into all kinds of new experiences. I lived through them—because Neil was right there for me.

Two more kids gave testimonies. I didn't hear the first because thoughts of Neil were once again racing through my mind.

After a lively discussion about something called the "fruit of the Spirit," we stood and formed a circle to pray. Some voiced specific concerns to the rest of the group who then individually prayed aloud for them. I was amazed at the way they prayed for one another. It seemed as if they really did care! I was surprised they didn't use a lot of fancy words like I'd heard preachers do on television. They just told God what they needed and then closed with "Amen."

On the few occasions I'd given the subject any thought, I'd always pictured Christianity as much more complicated than this.

"Anyone going to Tebo's?" Marc asked as everyone began moving around after prayer.

"It's so crowded there," Cheryl protested. "Let's go to my house and make pizza."

"Great idea," Grady agreed. "Is that okay with you, Andrea?"

I nodded apprehensively, wishing desperately that I could easily fake emotions and feelings instead of having my face constantly give me away. I didn't want to go to Cheryl's, and it certainly showed. If Grady could read my negative attitude, he didn't let on.

I did want to be with Grady, though. We waited for Cheryl while she was inviting everyone. I could see why Grady liked her. She was gracious, sweet, and composed.

She was everything I wasn't. I found myself watching closely for any crack in her perfection. Did she have big feet? No, they were petite. Maybe she dyed her hair that gorgeous reddish brown. If so, she covered her roots well.

"Her mother dropped her off," Grady told me as we waited. "I offered her a lift home."

*How nice of you,* I thought miserably.

"Ready?" She beamed at Grady when she'd finished her rounds. She proceeded to talk nonstop all the way to the car about whether to make Canadian bacon, pepperoni, or both.

When Grady opened the door for us, she scrambled in first and unlocked his side. He climbed in beside her and I watched her possessively place her hand on his knee, letting me know in short order that she had staked her claim and there would be no trespassing.

The words "take me home, please" formed on my tongue, but a newfound determination stopped them from being vocalized. *I want to get to know some of these people,* I thought. *Why should I let Cheryl stop me?* I reminded myself that Grady and I were nothing more than friends. I trusted him to make Cheryl understand that.

I would have enjoyed the evening if I could have taken my eyes off Grady and Cheryl. She refused to let him out of her sight. By asking his help in making the pizza and expecting him to serve it, she managed to keep him busy the entire evening. The few times he tried to involve me, Cheryl quickly reassured me that there wasn't much to do and I should just relax and have a good time.

Grady occasionally found his way over to me, checking to see if my Coke glass was empty or to make sure I had someone to talk to.

I didn't want more Coke, and I thought I'd scream if I had to struggle at making conversation with one more person. Although my original intention had been to try to get to know some of the group, all I really wanted was Grady's attention. I wanted him to sit with me for a while, to show his friends that I was someone important to him.

After being assured that I was taken care of, he always returned to Cheryl's side.

Jill Wagner seemed to be making an effort to be my friend. We played a couple of games of Ping-Pong together. When we sat down, she began asking me about Neil. I sensed immediately her genuine interest in me and started talking about my favorite subject.

"Accepting his death must have been hard for you," she said, after I'd told her everything in detail from how I met Neil to how we spent our last night together.

"I hope I never experience anything like it again," I admitted. "I'll always love him, but I'm hoping it will be a little easier now that I've become a Christian."

Jill eyed me sympathetically. "I believe it will. Jesus fills those empty spots in our lives." She reached over and hugged me. Christians were sure affectionate.

She then invited me to have lunch with her sometime at Tebo's restaurant where she worked part time. I wondered if Grady had put her up to all this friendliness.

Although I honestly tried to give my undivided attention to whomever I was talking to at the moment, my eyes kept glancing at Grady and Cheryl. They seemed so familiar with each other. I wondered how long they'd been dating.

When I saw her reach up and plant a quick kiss on his cheek, I mentally gave myself a little pep talk. *It doesn't matter. You don't care. They really make a nice couple. Grady deserves a sweet Christian girl like Cheryl.*

Unfortunately, I did care about Grady. It mattered very much. I needed his support. I wanted his full attention, and I didn't want this "nice Christian girl" to interfere.

I couldn't understand my mixed feelings. Retreating into a shell for the rest of the evening, I consciously set my thoughts on Neil. I wouldn't let anyone take his place in my heart, and that included Grady Hollinger.

# 7

$\mathscr{I}$commended myself on surviving the second week of existence without Neil. Another lonely, memory-filled weekend suddenly loomed ahead of me. In the past I'd lived for Neil's weekends home from school. Friends and activities had filled the time. Neil and I had spent every spare minute together until he begrudgingly departed on Sunday nights.

Now the same friends and activities continued despite the fact that the most important person was missing. The action even intensified because of summer, and I hated the very idea that normal life could carry on as if nothing had happened. Neil was the leader. He was the one who consistently kept things going.

I avoided our crowd as much as I could. Watching the happy couples caused me to go into a deeper loneliness. I couldn't understand why life had dealt me such a harsh blow. Everyone else had managed to pick up the pieces and move on, so why couldn't I?

I stayed by myself a lot and dreamed about happier times when Neil was still alive.

Chuck came over on Saturday night, and the three of us watched television together.

"I hear you're into God now," Chuck mentioned non-chalantly during a commercial.

"Into God?" I echoed. "I became a Christian, if that's what you mean."

"I used to be one." His eyes took on a faraway look. "It was right before I married Carolyn. When she died three years later, I gave up on everything—including God."

I stared hard at Chuck. I'd never known he'd been married before, let alone that he'd actually lived for God at one time. He must have loved his wife very much to become so bitter at God after her death. Maybe he could really understand where I was coming from.

"I know what you're going through right now," he went on. "It's not easy, is it? You're handling it a lot better than I did. If I had turned to God instead of away—"

My mother suddenly jumped up from the couch. "Let's make some popcorn, Chuck."

"Why, Sandra, if I didn't know you better, I'd think you were trying to change the subject." He winked at me, then followed her into the kitchen.

Good ol' Chuck. There was a caring person behind that handsome, fun-loving face. It must be hard for a man to lose his wife, possibly more difficult than it was for me to lose Neil. I could hardly imagine that. I wondered if Chuck had ever considered going back to God.

I didn't pursue the subject. I knew he'd talk more when he was ready.

As I set my alarm clock that night, I determined that nothing would keep me from church this time.

———

Grady looked pleased to see me the next morning. It made my efforts seem worthwhile. I enjoyed the music, and the pastor's sermon was easy to follow. I especially liked how close everyone seemed and how friendly they were.

When Grady invited me to join him and some others for lunch after the service, I refused. A replay of Thursday didn't appeal to me. I couldn't ignore the fact that he and

Cheryl were a couple, and I chose not to watch them in action.

Grady looked genuinely disappointed when I declined his invitation—so much so, that I almost changed my mind. But when I saw Cheryl hurrying toward us, I held to my first decision. "Thanks, anyway," I yelled over my shoulder as I made a quick exit.

I arrived home to find a note from my mother saying she'd gone for a ride with Chuck. I wandered around the empty house for a while, then decided to sit outside on the front porch and do my nails.

I'd been sitting there for about ten minutes when I heard a faint roaring in the distance. It sounded so much like Neil's bike that I set my nail polish down, closed my eyes, and replayed in my mind the familiar picture of Neil's arrival on his motorcycle. He'd looked so handsome dressed in his boots, gloves, and leather jacket. He'd take his goggles off and I'd run into his arms. . . .

The sound of the bike grew louder and I knew it was nearby. As the sound of the approaching bike increased, I opened my eyes just in time to see it turn into our driveway and stop a few feet away.

Drew cut the motor and took off his helmet. He hung it on the handlebars, climbed off, and strode casually up the driveway.

"Hi." He smiled. "You haven't been around much. I've missed you. Want to go for a ride?"

I stared at Drew and then at his bike. I had decided that I would never ride a motorcycle again, but given the opportunity, I knew that Neil would want me to accept.

"I'll get my helmet." I ran into the house and grabbed my helmet from the hall closet.

As I climbed on the bike behind Drew, a sudden fear swept over me. *I'm crazy,* I told myself as he revved the engine. Here I am on the back of a motorcycle with a near stranger only two weeks after Neil's death because of one.

What was I afraid of? The worst thing that could happen would be that we crash, and I would die and then go to heaven to be with Neil. I relaxed slightly thinking about the possibility of being with Neil again.

"Ready?" Drew yelled.

"Ready!" I returned.

We zoomed down the driveway and into the street. I closed my eyes and fantasized about wrapping my arms around Neil's waist instead of Drew's. The wind whipped through my shirt and hit my uncovered face whenever I peeked around Drew to see where we were going. I loved it!

Drew steered the bike expertly into the entrance of McGiver Park and stopped under an elm tree. Neil and I had visited this park whenever we wanted to be alone, which was fairly often. It was spread out over at least fifty square city blocks and had many private paths on which to hike and explore.

"Is it getting any better?" Drew asked kindly as we walked along the main trail.

I shrugged. "I don't know. The hours and minutes just kind of run together. How about you?"

"It's tough, isn't it? Everything seems kind of dead. No matter what we try to do as a group, it falls apart without Neil around to hold it together."

"You feel that way too? I thought I was the only one who really missed him."

"Don't forget that we lived together at school. I saw him every day. He wouldn't want you pulling away from our group, you know. We all need each other."

I thought about what he was saying, but didn't respond.

When we reached the lake, Drew pulled a small bag from the pocket of his jacket. He handed the bag of bread crumbs to me. Flocks of ducks appeared everywhere. We emptied the bag in a matter of seconds. Sitting down on the bank, Drew pulled another small bag and some cigarette papers from his other pocket. He began sprinkling the dried weed onto the paper.

"It's good stuff," he said. "Acapulco Gold."

I didn't want to smoke dope with him. I wished just once my crowd could do something without getting stoned. How was I going to handle this without hurting his feelings?

He lit it, took a long drag, and held it out to me.

I slowly shook my head. "No thank you."

*Here we go again,* I thought. *A reenactment of the scene with Nancy and Terri.*

He frowned. "Why not?"

After taking off my sandals, I lowered my feet into the cool water. It would be so easy to accept Drew's offer and float away into nowhere land for a few hours. Today, if I chose, I could rise above my problems, forgetting about everything and everyone who demanded that I be real. I could remain, for a short period of time, in a dimension where pain ended and life became a comedy. When I was high, I usually moved from one laughing spell to the next.

"C'mon, don't be boring." Drew continued to hold the joint out to me.

It looked inviting, but now I had to consider what God wanted me to do. Is this the way He wanted me to handle life? Did He want me to run from one joint to the next, taking in smoke every time I couldn't cope? Besides, nothing ever changed. Even though for a while I uncaringly laughed my problems away, I eventually came crashing down to the same hurts, the same people, and the same unhappy me. I still had to deal with the same problems or else smoke another joint to forget about them again.

What I felt for Neil now couldn't really even be described as pain. Since meeting Christ, the intensity of the hurt had changed. Inside, I had a new hope that I would see him again.

"I don't need to escape today," I told Drew. "I think I can handle it."

"Really?" Drew arched his brows. "I would think Neil's death would make you want to get away from it more than ever."

Did I have to go through another person's ridicule of my faith in God? Anything less than honesty and boldness would be copping out on God.

"A few days ago I needed to escape, but you see I've . . . uh . . . I've found a different way to deal with life."

Drew nodded knowingly. "You've been holding out on us. Let's see it. Is it something I haven't tried?"

He thought I was referring to a new kind of dope. I swallowed uncomfortably.

"You can't exactly see it. It's called God."

He slowly lifted his head, his eyes piercing mine. "God? Grady's thing, huh?"

"Yeah."

"Wow!" He put the joint to his lips, inhaled deeply, held his breath, and slowly breathed out. We didn't talk as he finished his cigarette. Uncrossing his legs, he got up and motioned for me to follow him. Together, we began to climb one of the trails that took us deeper into a secluded wooded area of the park.

"So is this God thing helping you?" Drew asked as we walked.

"You might say that. It hasn't been that long."

Another uncomfortable silence. Drew seemed to be a real thinker.

Suddenly we stopped and he turned to face me. He was so close that I stepped back, but a huge tree stood right behind me. Placing an arm on each side of me, his eyes met mine in a questioning gaze.

"Can I be completely honest with you about something?" he asked.

"Sure," I gulped. Did I have a choice? I couldn't move in any direction.

"You're really a great girl," he began. "I mean, I like you—a lot. I guess I did even when Neil was around."

"You did?"

"Yep. And I'm having a hard time right now trying to keep from doing this."

Before I knew what was happening, his arms were around me and his lips were on mine. I pushed at his chest with all my might. He released me instantly, and I scrambled around him and up the trail a few feet. I stood and glared at him.

"You're mad!" He looked ashamed. "I'm sorry. You said I could be honest."

"Not *that* honest," I lashed out. "Whatever gave you the impression that I—"

"Neil said once that you—" He stopped in the middle of his sentence. "Never mind. Hey, I'm sorry, okay?"

"Neil said what?"

"I said never mind," he spoke sharply. "I shouldn't have done it. It was just what I felt like doing at the moment."

We started back down the trail the way we'd come.

"Do you always do what you feel like doing?"

He nodded. "Most of the time. Unless someone like you comes along and ruins it for me."

"Are you an only child, Drew?"

"Yeah. How did you know?"

"Because you're a spoiled brat, just like me."

It was true, I suppose. I liked having my own way, and when something happened that I didn't like, I became terribly frustrated. When Neil died, I was angry because his death had completely wrecked my perfect plans for life.

"So we're both spoiled brats. We have something in common."

I smiled. "Big deal."

"Hey, I'm glad to see that smile. It means you're not mad at me anymore."

"Just don't try it again."

"I'll try my hardest not to."

*Something about Drew appeals to me,* I thought during the ride home. Apparently something about me appealed to him too. For his sake, I hoped he would back off, because Neil took up every ounce of room in my heart. No room remained for Drew or anyone else—except maybe Grady. He was so much like Neil, but he also had something different about him that I wanted to get to know.

I thanked Drew for the ride, assured him there were no hard feelings, and entered the house to find my mother and Chuck sitting at the dining room table drinking coffee.

"Who was that?" Mom asked.

"Drew Bradshaw. He and Neil roomed together at college."

"So you're not sitting around grieving for Neil," Chuck put in.

"I am grieving for Neil," I retorted. "I just do it wherever I am." I grabbed a handful of taco chips out of the bowl on the table. "I think I'll go over to Terri's. See you later."

As I jogged the three blocks to her house, I found myself wondering what Grady did on Sunday afternoons.

I had reacted so violently to Drew's kiss. Would I have responded the same way to Grady? Probably so. It just repulsed me to be touched by any guy other than Neil. Would it always be this way? Would there ever come a time when I would want to date seriously again, to love and be loved? I couldn't even bear to look that far ahead.

Terri seemed glad to see me and led me down to the family room in the basement, which stayed cool during the hot summer days. I flopped down on a floor pillow and kicked off my shoes while Terri spread out on the couch across from me.

"Drew took me for a ride on his motorcycle today," I said.

"He did? Weren't you afraid to ride after Neil's accident?"

"At first. But I'm glad I went. I felt safe with him. He handles his bike pretty well."

I decided not to mention the kiss. She'd tell Nancy, and then in a matter of hours, the *National Enquirer* would be wanting our story. I was sure that Nancy would blow the whole incident out of proportion.

"It was just a friendly ride, then?" Terri wanted to know.

"Yeah, I guess you could say that."

"You don't really feel like dating, do you?"

"No."

"I can tell. I don't blame you. If I lost Rich, I'd never want to date anyone else. I guess I'd stay an old maid all my life."

"Dating turns me off, but the thought of being alone terrifies me even more."

"You don't have to be alone." Terri sat up straight and tucked her legs under her. "We've really missed you the last couple of weeks. We not only lost Neil, but we seem to be losing you too."

"I'm sorry. I didn't think anyone really cared if I was there or not. Actually, I've lost my incentive to go anywhere or be with anyone. Without Neil, I'm not sure I even know how to have fun."

"Hey, I understand." Terri jumped up from the couch. "Maybe you're just going to have to force yourself for a while. Let's start by going to Smitty's and getting a Coke. I'll bet you haven't been there once in the last two weeks."

Smitty's was the local hangout, a hamburger joint that sucked kids in its doors faster than it could spit them back out. The walls of the building bulged while kids stood around drinking Cokes, playing pool or video games, or just talking with one another. I avoided Smitty's because I knew I'd feel lonelier in that crowd than I would at home.

Somehow I let myself be talked into going. We hopped into Terri's mother's sedan and headed for Smitty's. I found myself wondering if Drew would be there. We passed the church and I noticed a few people standing outside, some on their way inside.

"Hey, wait a minute," I ordered. "Stop the car."

Terri looked confused, but pulled off the road.

"The evening service at Grady's church is beginning in a few minutes. Let's go and you can see firsthand what I'm in to."

I was sure that once Terri was confronted with the person of Jesus Christ, as I was, she would jump in with both feet. I just didn't know enough yet to give her a good picture of Him myself.

"Are you kidding? I don't want to go to church."

"C'mon, you'll like it. It's not boring like a lot of churches. The pastor just talks to us out of the Bible. If you don't like it, we'll leave."

"But I've only got jeans—"

"They don't care what you look like in this church. We'll sit in the back anyway."

"Listen, I haven't been to a church service in my entire life except for a couple of weddings and funerals. I wouldn't want to break my record."

"I'm going to Smitty's with you," I pouted.

"Oh—okay, okay," Terri muttered as she made a U-turn and drove back toward the church. "If you tell Nancy about this, I'll never speak to you again."

The congregation was already singing as we slipped into the back row. I scanned every pew, looking for Grady. I'd about given up when I finally saw him sitting against the wall on the other side of the church. He smiled when our eyes met. Blushing, I turned away. He had probably watched me look for him. I felt anger stir inside of me as I noticed Cheryl playing with a button on his jacket. Why did it matter? I missed Neil so much. Maybe these jealous feelings were stirred up because Grady resembled him in so many ways. Watching Grady with Cheryl was like seeing Neil with another girl. Whatever the reason, I suddenly wished Cheryl's family would get the urge to move again.

I watched Terri during the service; she seemed to be enjoying herself. She even clapped along with the rest of us during a song that the choir sang. She listened attentively to Pastor Thorsen's message. He preached on David and the significance of daily repentance and cleansing in our lives. He made it so simple, I knew Terri couldn't have missed it.

We left before they'd finished the closing song. I didn't feel like making small talk with Grady and Cheryl. Since he'd acknowledged my presence, I was sure he would feel obligated to talk to me after the service.

"What did you think?" I asked eagerly as we drove toward Smitty's.

"It was a nice service."

I wasn't about to let her get off that easy.

"What the pastor said tonight is for everyone, Terri," I began. "Jesus died for you too."

Terri nodded. "I know that, but I'm not sure I need Him like you do, Andrea. I've got Rich, and I'm satisfied with my life. I think it's great for you—really I do."

"What if you weren't satisfied? I mean, being satisfied isn't really the issue, is it? It's whether Jesus died for us or not. I believe He did."

My words hung suspended in the air as we pulled into the parking lot and climbed out of the car. I knew Terri would think about them.

We walked into Smitty's, and before we even made it to an empty table at least five people had asked me where I'd been. They had missed me.

Terri and I chose a table in the back. I quietly listened to the laughter around the room. People moved about exchanging phone numbers, discussing where they would meet that evening.

I sat wondering if the youth group had gone to Tebo's after the service. Was Grady holding Cheryl's hand at this moment? Were they snuggled cozily together in a booth?

"Where are you?" Terri's voice penetrated my thoughts.

"Huh? Nowhere. I'm back now."

The waitress brought our Cokes and I stirred mine with a straw thoughtfully, all the while watching everyone around me.

"It's all so shallow, Terri."

She looked puzzled.

"This." I motioned to the noisy activity going on around me. "What's the point? At the end of the evening you're broke and what have you gained? A higher score. Big deal."

Terri still looked confused. "Why do you have to gain anything?"

"Life has to have some meaning to it—a purpose. Do you want to have lived your life in vain?"

"What's with you, Andrea? I'm only seventeen years old. I'm having too much fun to think about meaning and purpose and all that serious stuff. I'll worry about that when I'm old."

I sighed. "You sound like Nancy. By the time you get old, it'll be too late. It really wouldn't hurt you to at least try it."

"Try what?"

"Christianity. You won't be sorry."

Terri frowned. "Nancy said it would be like this with you, but I didn't believe her. Lay off for a while, will you? You'll be the first to know if I ever decide I need God. Okay?"

"Yeah, sure. I'm sorry. I didn't realize I was being pushy."

"That's okay. Just give me a little room. Because of what happened to Neil, you may find yourself trying a lot of new things in order to help you cope." She leaned back and lit a cigarette. "I want you to be happy. I really do. Just understand that I'm not where you are. Someday I might be. There may come a time when I do need God; you never know."

I nodded. No one could really understand another person's pain. Sure, Terri missed Neil too, but there was no way she could fully comprehend the degree of hurt that I'd suffered. She may never know that pain.

As long as life was good to Terri, she'd possibly never feel her need for God.

I made a mental note to keep quiet about this in the future. I would let her come to me on her own when she was ready.

In the meantime, I would pray for her as someone must have prayed for me.

To that person, I would be eternally grateful.

# 8

At youth meeting on Thursday evening, Jill Wagner once again invited me to meet her for lunch at Tebo's. We decided to meet at eleven-thirty the next day. I looked forward to any conversation not revolving around dope, boyfriends, or parties.

Jill, a warm, friendly, outgoing person, seemed to be making a concentrated effort to get to know me. She stayed close by my side at church and youth meetings, making small talk or introducing me to someone new. I wanted to get to know her better.

As I waited for her to join me in a corner booth that warm Friday morning, I noticed that many of the customers were on a first-name basis with the waitresses. Jill fit right in.

"Mr. Sandstrom, you sure do look handsome in that blue suit," I overheard her tell an elderly gentleman at the table next to me. She laughed easily. I could tell that she knew how to make people feel special.

Hanging her apron on a nearby hook, she approached my table and slid gracefully onto the seat across from me.

She smiled. "Hi. Have you looked at the menu? Order whatever you want. It's on me."

"No, I can—"

"I insist," Jill interrupted. "My dad's the manager."

A waitress took our order. I glanced uneasily at Jill, wondering what we would have in common to talk about? We hardly knew each other.

"Well, what's it like being a new Christian?" Jill asked. "It's been eleven years since I accepted Christ."

"I'm learning a lot of new things," I told her. "I've really enjoyed being around you and the others at youth group. Sometimes I feel torn because my close friends don't understand, and I'm always on the defensive with them."

Jill nodded. "It will probably be a while before they start taking you seriously. That's one reason hanging around us will help. You need to have one group of friends who don't think you're crazy and who can strengthen and encourage you. Grady is so proud of you. He's glad for how you accepted Jesus into your life so quickly. He hardly talks about anything else."

My heart flipped momentarily. Though I loved Neil and he'd been gone only a short time, I found myself being drawn more and more to Grady. I was glad he was proud of me.

I faked a yawn. "Oh, really?"

"Yeah. He talks about you all the time. If it wasn't for Cheryl, you'd probably see more of him."

"Do you really think so?" I blurted, blowing my cool cover.

Jill nodded. "Cheryl's parents and Grady's parents have been friends for years. The Rileys moved away for a while, and when they moved back, Mrs. Hollinger and Mrs. Riley wasted no time in getting Grady and Cheryl together. I'm not sure Grady likes her all that much."

"You don't think so?"

A short, balding man approached our booth and set hamburgers down in front of us.

"I don't want to rush you," he said to Jill. "But try not to take longer than an hour. I need you."

"Sure, Dad. This is Andrea Lyons. She's the one I told you about—the one who used to date Neil Hollinger." She turned to me. "Andrea, this is my father."

"Pleased to meet you, Andrea." Mr. Wagner clasped my hand in his. "I hope you don't get the wrong impression of me. I'm not a slavedriver. It's just that I had to fire a girl this morning and we're short of help. Say, are you interested in a job?"

"I, uh, well—yeah, maybe so."

It hadn't occurred to me to work this summer. I'd planned on spending every free minute with Neil. Now that greatly anticipated free time was nearly driving me up the wall. I was bored and lonely. I remembered how Mom was always griping because she had to give me money. Yeah, a job might be just what I needed.

"When you're finished eating, why don't you come to my office and fill out an application?"

"Okay."

As he left, Jill squeezed my arm. "Wouldn't that be great?" she exclaimed. "We could have a lot of fun working together this summer." She bit into her hamburger, chewing thoughtfully. "Have you had any experience?"

"Not much. Just a few days of working at a drive-in last summer."

"I've already given you a high character reference. There's not that much to learn."

Jill heartily waved to someone out the window behind me. I turned to see Grady and Marc Steele walking toward the building. I almost choked on my hamburger, but quickly regained my composure before Jill noticed. What was it about Grady that made me so nervous? My heart was beating rapidly, but I wasn't exactly sure why. He wasn't Neil; he was only his little brother.

I watched him move through the door toward us with an innocent, boyish look on his face. His shoulders were squared and he walked confidently.

Jill scooted over to let Marc slide in beside her, and Grady slipped in next to me. When his arm touched mine,

I felt my knees go weak. *This is crazy,* I thought. *It was just an arm; why did he have this effect on me?*

"Sorry, Marc," Jill began. "I took my break early. But you guys are just in time. We need to pray about something. My dad offered Andrea a job, but she still has to fill out the application."

"Terrific!" Grady exclaimed. "You'll like working here. The food's the best in town, and Mr. Wagner is great to work for. I worked here last summer."

"I haven't landed the job yet," I couldn't help reminding them.

"Let's take care of that now," Marc offered, his eyes twinkling.

I liked Marc. He had a boyish innocence about him, making it easy to talk to him and trust him. It was relaxing to be with Christians after I had felt so uneasy with my old friends.

We held hands around the table. I struggled to keep my hand that Grady held steady. It would be awful if he knew how he affected me. Grady prayed softly that God would touch Mr. Wagner's heart to give me the job.

"Thanks a lot," I said when he had finished his prayer.

Everyone let go of hands, but when I started to pull my hand out of Grady's, he grinned and tightened his grip.

"Marc and I work around the corner at Ed's Automotive Shop," Grady said. "We get discounts on car parts. I'm rebuilding the engine in my '69 Mustang, and the discount sure comes in handy."

"How nice," I said. And how convenient. I was beginning to like the idea of this job more and more.

Jill pushed her plate in front of Marc. "You can finish my hamburger. I see my dad looking over here. He had to fire a girl this morning, so he's short on help." She lowered her voice. "I think God definitely had his hand in this one, because I had no idea she was going to get fired when I asked Andrea to meet me for lunch."

Marc rose to let Jill get by him. "I'll see you tonight," he told her.

She nodded, then turned to me. "I enjoyed having lunch with you, Andrea. I'll talk to you later."

She hurried off.

"I'd better go talk to Mr. Wagner," I said.

"What's the hurry?" Grady asked. "Stick around. I never get to talk to you. You always run out of church."

"Have you heard of the telephone?" I shot back, then immediately bit my tongue. *Why did I say that?* It might sound too much like I'd been waiting for him to call me.

Marc grinned. "Yep, you got him there. I like your spunk."

"I didn't mean—"

"No, you're right," Grady interrupted. "I should have at least called by now to see how you're getting along."

"How *are* you doing?" Marc asked.

"Okay," I answered.

Marc, a deeply sensitive guy, noticed my feeble attempt to respond graciously to Grady's question.

"Are you sure?" he asked gently.

"Well, I'm feeling like—I don't belong anywhere," I blurted out. "My friends don't understand me anymore, and it's so hard to get to know the kids at church."

Grady sighed. "I suppose that's my fault too. I should be getting you involved in our youth activities. Are you going on the hayride?"

I shrugged. "I don't know." Everyone would be paired up and no one had asked me.

"You don't know if you're going?" Grady repeated. "You mean, you don't have a date? I'll see what I can do about that."

I was about to tell him not to bother, that he owed me no favors; yet, I really did want to go. It would be a good opportunity to get to know some of the other kids.

"I'd better go now," I said.

"If you have to." Grady moved to let me out. "Let me know if you get the job."

I promised I would.

Mr. Wagner's door was open and he motioned for me to come in.

"Hi, Andrea." He smiled warmly. "Sit down."

I sat down in the chair beside his desk and realized that I was a bit nervous.

"I'll have you fill out an application and then we'll talk." He handed me a two-page form. "I'll be back in a few minutes."

I methodically began to write in the answers to the questions. As I glanced over the application, all hope of filling the position diminished.

My previous employment was not impressive. The seven-day job I'd held at the drive-in the previous summer seemed hardly worth mentioning. My mind had been everywhere except on my responsibility. Neil had put in his appearance the day I started and continued to hang around every day after that. I should have quit that first day because it was absolutely impossible to divide myself between him and my customers.

I never did figure out why he even noticed me when so many girls had tried to get his attention during the school year. Being only a sophomore, I admired him from a distance, as did most of my friends. Maybe since it was summer, age didn't matter as much. Or maybe away from the competition of so many others, his choices were more clearcut. When we started dating, I quit work so I'd be available whenever he asked me out. Those first dates were really special. Before I knew what had happened, I'd fallen head over heels for Neil Hollinger. Nothing else seemed to matter—school, friends, sports, nothing. . . .

Mr. Wagner returned, interrupting my thoughts. Luckily, I had just finished filling out the last question before my mind had wandered off.

Mr. Wagner scanned my application, frowning slightly. "I should accept more applications because you don't have much experience, but since my daughter speaks so highly of you and I trust her judgment, I'll give you a chance. Can you be here tomorrow at 8:00 A.M.?"

"Yes, sir."

"You can call me Jack." He rose. "I'll see you in the morning."

"Thank you—thank you very much."

I opened the door to leave and Jill practically fell into the room.

"Eavesdropping a little?" Mr. Wagner asked as he walked by us.

"Just thought I'd say goodbye to Andrea," Jill answered. When he was out of earshot, she said, "I knew you'd get it. Now, don't worry about a thing. God helped you get this job and He'll help you learn fast. In one week no one will be able to tell you haven't worked here all your life."

"I hope so," I said, and thanked her for helping me get the job.

As I walked out, I glanced over to the table where I'd left Grady and Marc. They were gone.

Outside, I stood for a moment waiting for my eyes to adjust to the bright sunlight. Then I saw a motorcycle parked at the curb. There stood Drew leaning against the front tire, his arms crossed in front of his chest.

"Hi, beautiful. You've kept me waiting. Your mom said you'd be here, but I didn't see you inside."

"I was in the back, applying for a job. I got it too."

"A job?" Drew looked disgusted. "What for?"

I shrugged. "There's nothing else going on this summer. Besides, I need the money."

"Hey, I can think of lots of things to do this summer. Most of them don't cost much." He smiled crookedly.

I didn't know exactly what he meant, and I wasn't sure I wanted to know.

"If Neil were still around, you wouldn't even consider working. Why don't you run in and tell them you've changed your mind. No one—I mean, no one is working this summer." He leaned over and patted me under the chin. "Girl, you get some crazy ideas sometimes."

Drew was right. I'd probably be the only one in our crowd working this summer. I wasn't as much a part of the group anymore, but if I let him, Drew would be quick to pull me back into the middle of the action. Apparently, he was just waiting for me to give him the green light so he could make his entrance into my closed world.

"We really miss your pretty face," Drew went on. "I keep telling them this religion thing will pass and you'll be back."

"Don't be so sure," I answered. He didn't seem to hear me and seemed distracted by something behind me.

I turned to see Grady jogging toward us. *Now what should I do?* This could be a very uncomfortable moment if I didn't handle it right.

If I had any idea whatsoever that they would be hostile toward each other because of me, I couldn't have been more wrong.

"Hey, you got a new paint job." Grady ran his hand over the body of Drew's bike. "That's a great-looking shade of blue."

"Thanks. I wish Neil could have seen it. He's the one who kept telling me to get one."

The bike talk continued as they discussed the engine, the pipes, and the instrument panel. As they began to examine the automatic starter, Grady suddenly looked at his watch.

"Oh—I've got to get back to work." He turned to me. "I just—took a break to see if you got the job."

"I start tomorrow."

"All right! I thought you would. Well, I gotta get back. I'll see you two later."

He turned and quickly jogged down the sidewalk. He didn't even act the least bit jealous of Drew.

Drew shook his head. "Straight, really straight. Nothing like Neil, huh?"

"He's okay," I defended.

"For a Hollinger," he smirked. "About that job . . ."

"I'm going to give it a try," I told him bluntly.

Grady had taken a personal interest in whether or not I got this job. I couldn't disappoint him. After all, we had prayed and God had answered. I couldn't turn my back on God's answer to prayer.

Drew looked surprised, then shrugged. "I can't run your life for you."

*You'll give it your best shot, though,* I thought matter-of-factly. Maybe that's exactly what I needed—someone to run my life. I found it extremely difficult making the most simple decisions since Neil had died.

"You'll be sorry when you see us caravan past this place on our way to the beach." He grinned. "What I really came over to ask you is if you'd like to go with me to a party Friday night."

"Friday night?"

I was so tired of staying home night after night. It might be fun to be with the crowd again.

I suddenly remembered the hayride. I wanted to leave that night open just in case someone asked me.

"I think I have plans," I hedged.

"You *think*?"

"I'm pretty sure. I'm sorry."

"The party is at Peter Kahlberg's. If your plans fall

through, I'll be there." He hopped on his bike and gunned the engine. "We're really going to have to get together."

I nodded and watched his bike until it was out of sight. Drew was a nice guy. These last few weeks had been lonely ones. I wondered if Neil would want me to date again. God had definitely filled a large void in my life, but I couldn't help feeling the need to touch someone—a flesh-and-blood someone.

What would Neil want? That was really what it all boiled down to. Would he want me to love again? Or would he want me to stay loyal to him? What about my attraction to Grady? Would Neil approve?

# 9

*J*ill saw me the minute I entered the restaurant the next day and hurried over to meet me. She immediately began to drill me on the mechanics of waitressing. I followed her around all morning, learning some basics about serving tables and dealing with customers, even difficult ones.

One old man made us return his eggs four times before he was satisfied. Another lady kept us running back and forth refilling her coffee cup when it didn't look to me like she'd even taken one sip. Jill remained gracious and always complied with their wishes, even smiling while doing so.

The morning passed quickly. I was watching Jill work the cash register when Grady and Marc entered the restaurant.

As usual, my heart began to race and my stomach felt like it was full of butterflies.

"This cash register is really temperamental," Jill was saying. "You have to hit it on the left side like this to get it open. Then you kind of pull on this end . . ."

Grady wore blue jeans and a khaki green shirt. He saw me and waved.

I raised my arm in return, but my movement was as rigid as the drawer on the cash register. I wanted so much to look natural and nonchalant.

Jill looked up. "Hey, you're not even listening to me."

"I'm sorry, Jill, I—"

"Oh, I see. Marc and Grady. Forget about the cash register. I'll show you later. Let's take our lunch break." She led the way to the corner booth that the guys had chosen. "Get out your pad and pencil," she added over her shoulder. "You can take our order."

I stood in front of Grady and tried to steady my pad in my shaky left hand while holding a pencil firmly in my right.

"I'll have a chef salad." He smiled up at me as I wrote down his order.

I turned to Marc.

"Hey, aren't you forgetting something?" Grady asked, a teasing look in his eyes. "You're supposed to ask me what kind of dressing I'd like."

"I just assumed you wanted French," I told him. "It's what Neil always ordered."

"I'm not Neil," Grady said, the teasing expression now gone. "I don't like French. I'd like Thousand Island dressing, please."

Why had I said that? Of course he wasn't Neil. He didn't have to like French dressing just because it was Neil's favorite.

I hurriedly wrote down a salad for Jill and cheeseburgers for Marc and myself. I made a quick exit, trying not to burst into tears. Why did I do such stupid things?

I decided to wait in the kitchen until our order came up.

"I'll bring it out," Jack offered as he flipped the burgers.

I had no excuse to hang around the kitchen. I might as well get out there and see if I could undo the damage already done.

As I rejoined them, they were laughing and talking like they'd completely forgotten about it.

I wondered where Cheryl was today. What would she think if she walked in right now?

"Let's take a walk down to the fountain," Grady suggested to me when we'd finished eating.

Jill looked at her watch. "You've got exactly fifteen minutes. Walk fast."

That was like telling a hummingbird to slow down. I don't think Grady knew how to walk fast. At least *I'd* never seen him do so.

The sun's rays burned into our backs as we walked the five blocks to the fountain. We reached our destination and found the cool spray in the air a welcome and refreshing change from the scorching heat.

Grady seemed preoccupied as we circled the fountain and then headed back toward the restaurant.

"I hope the weather stays nice," I said, trying to make conversation.

"Uh-huh," he mumbled and then said, "You know, I really want to go on that hayride on Friday. Would you like to go?"

"You're kidding. With you?"

He looked hurt. "Well, yeah, I mean—"

"Oh, I didn't mean that I wouldn't want to go with you," I added quickly. "You just took me by surprise. I thought, well, never mind—I'd love to go with you."

"Are you sure?" He still looked confused.

"Of course I'm sure."

"Good." He acted relieved, like he had been sure I would refuse his invitation. "Hey, I've got a straw hat from Mexico that I can wear. And I'll wear my overalls."

"I can wear my hair in pigtails," I said. His enthusiasm was contagious. "I'll borrow one of Chuck's plaid shirts and wear it with my overalls."

As we planned our evening, I began to get really excited about the hayride. I hadn't been able to admit to myself how much I hoped to go. I didn't know any other guys in the youth group well enough to expect one of them to take me. I never dreamed that Grady would ask me himself. I just assumed he would be taking Cheryl. I wondered why he wasn't.

Grady and I returned to our jobs, and I didn't get to tell Jill about his invitation until our break late that afternoon.

"I knew he was going to ask you," she said.

"I took it for granted he'd be taking Cheryl."

"She's on vacation for the next two weeks."

"Oh, I see."

"He would have asked you anyway," she quickly added. "Marc says he's feeling a little closed in. He needs some air." She smiled. "You don't mind if he breathes in your direction, do you?"

"Not at all," I returned thoughtfully. I had two whole weeks without Cheryl to worry about. A lot could happen in two weeks.

---

Terri and Nancy dropped by my house that evening. We stayed outside on the front porch because Chuck was over, and conversation often became extremely exhausting with him around. He constantly butted in with stupid jokes and innuendos.

"You're going to Pete's party, aren't you?" Nancy asked.

"No. I'm going on a hayride with Grady."

"A hayride?" she echoed. "I suppose it's with your church."

I nodded.

"I don't believe this," Nancy remarked. "Pete's party is going to be a blast, and you'd rather sit in the hay with a bunch of religious nuts."

"Let's go to Smitty's," Terri suggested.

I was tired from working all day, and I wasn't feeling up to arguing with them, so I tagged along.

When I saw Drew standing in the doorway at Smitty's among a group of guys, I realized I should have settled for the argument with Terri and Nancy. At least I'd be at home right now instead of headed for more pressure from Drew about Pete's party.

Maybe we could slide by the guys without being noticed. No such luck.

"How're your 'not so sure' plans for Friday night?" Drew called out as he broke away from his friends. "They still on?"

I nodded.

"What are you doing? I can't think of anything more exciting than Pete's party."

Nancy laughed. "How about a church hayride?"

"Really? A hayride? Is she putting me on?"

I felt myself beginning to simmer. What was so incredible about a hayride? I was getting tired of always having to defend my actions. Weren't these my friends? Don't true friends let you be yourself? The minute I wanted to break out of their mold and do something that didn't have their stamp of approval, they branded me as weird and straight. I decided to walk back home by myself.

Turning to face Drew who still blocked the doorway, I said, "Excuse me."

"What do you mean, excuse me?" Drew returned. "Hey, don't get mad. A hayride might be fun. It's just that I couldn't picture Neil on a hay wagon and I figured that you—"

"Neil wouldn't be caught dead on a hayride," I interrupted angrily. "But Neil let me be myself. If I wanted to do something different, even if it seemed crazy, he never stopped me." I glared at Nancy. "And he never laughed at me."

Drew nodded. "You're right. I'm sorry. It seems like I'm always apologizing to you for something." He took my arm and led me to a table in the back of the room. Nancy, Terri, and the rest of Drew's friends followed. No one mentioned the hayride again. They spent the next half hour deciding how much beer to buy for Friday night, who to invite and who not to invite, and all kinds of boring details about something in which I had no interest.

If Neil had been here, and if I hadn't become a Christian, I suppose the conversation would have interested me. It didn't appeal to me anymore. I should have known better and stayed home.

The last few times I'd been with Terri and Nancy, we just didn't seem to have as much in common anymore. They lived from one party to the next, never stopping long enough to realize that there might be more to life than parties and getting high. I didn't know for sure whether it was Neil's death or my relationship with God that had changed the way I felt inside. All I knew was that we were headed in opposite directions. I didn't want to lose my friends, but I had no idea how to stop the separating process I realized was beginning to take place. I could no longer be who they wanted me to be. I could only be me—a person who had to express the way I felt inside instead of riding along with the tide of the crowd. Why did that seem so difficult?

*Neil, I wish you were here,* my heart cried among all the confusion in my mind. *Life has suddenly become so complicated without you.*

After an hour or so of idle chatter, Nancy and Terri took me home. Chuck and my mother were sitting at the dining room table playing Scrabble when I entered the room.

" 'Innate' is spelled with two n's," Mom told Chuck.

"Oh, hi, Andrea. You sure do come home early these days."

"We just went to Smitty's."

"How's the Christian life?" Chuck asked.

"Fine, thanks."

"I'd like to visit your church sometime. Where is it?"

Was he joking? I couldn't tell. I gave him the address in case he wasn't.

"Maybe your mother would go with me. How about it, Sandra? Church wouldn't hurt us."

Mom shook her head. "No thanks. That's not for me. Everything's going fine. I don't need religion."

"It's not religion," I began. "It's—"

"I know, I know." She cut me off, then turned to Chuck, "She always corrects me. It's not religion, but 'a relationship with Jesus Christ.' Well, I'll remember that if I ever need it. But right now, I've got a sweet daughter, a lovely home, and a handsome man. What do I need God for?"

"Your daughter may leave home someday." Chuck winked at me. "Houses catch on fire. And your handsome man may find another woman. Don't get nervous. He hasn't, but he might. What then?"

*All right, Chuck. Lay it on her. Not bad for a guy who isn't even living for God.*

"If those things ever happen, I may have to fall down on my knees and ask God for mercy," she quipped.

Chuck jumped up. "Get the matches, Andrea! We'll start with the house."

She smiled. "Could we finish this game first? I'm winning and it might be a sin for Christians to play Scrabble."

"What?" I laughed.

"You quit drinking," she went on. "You don't stay out until wee hours of the morning. You don't swear. You're not much fun anymore. Have you stopped smoking?"

"I'm working on it," I returned. "But I still play *Scrabble.*"

"Glad to hear it. Would you please run along now and let us finish our game?"

"Say a prayer for me," Chuck called as I turned and left the room.

I wish I knew when I could take Chuck seriously. In spite

of my prejudices toward my mother's boyfriends, I had to admit I liked Chuck and hoped he'd stick around for a while. He'd lasted longer than some of the others. They had been seeing each other for almost a year.

I assumed that my mother would have told me if Grady had called. I looked forward to having lunch with him the next day.

He didn't show up for lunch on Wednesday or on Thursday. Maybe he couldn't afford to eat out every day. Still, if he wanted to see me, he wouldn't mind spending the money.

Marc didn't come either, and Jill didn't seem worried. Of course, they were sure of each other's feelings. I didn't ask her about Grady. I didn't want him to find out that I was interested or concerned.

I finally saw him at our youth group meeting on Thursday night.

"I saved you a place." He patted the cushion beside him on the couch.

He stayed by my side all evening. I savored every minute of his attention, knowing that when Cheryl returned, I would soon be forgotten. It frustrated me. I never knew where I stood with Grady. Neil and I hadn't played this game. I didn't know the rules.

Grady walked me to the car after the meeting.

I automatically began to count the sprinkling of stars across the summer sky. It was one game Neil and I had played. We spent many nights lying out in my backyard counting stars.

We played "imagine" games. "Imagine if you and I were the only people alone on the planet. What would we do?" The ending to this game was predictable. We always ended up in each other's arms.

Grady touched my shoulder, bringing me back to reality.

"I'm looking forward to tomorrow night," he said, pulling his hand away. "I would really like to get to know you. You're one complex person, and I'm doing my best to understand you."

"I don't know if that's possible. I don't understand myself."

"If we put our heads together, maybe we can figure you out," he said with a laugh.

I doubted that, but I wouldn't discourage him from trying.

I suspected Grady would drop by the next day for lunch, but he didn't. Jill must have sensed that it bothered me. She assured me that the two guys were probably working on Grady's car. The day passed slowly. Finally it came to an end and I hurried home to dress for my date with Grady.

"Where are you going?" my mother asked.

"On a hayride with Grady."

"It's nice to see you doing something fun for a change. It seems like all you've done lately is work and go to church."

"Nothing's much fun without Neil," I mumbled.

"I believe it. Grady doesn't seem half as exciting."

"He's okay, but he's not Neil." I wasn't about to tell her how I felt. I tied a bow on the last pigtail and I backed away from the mirror to get a better look. "What are you and Chuck doing tonight?"

"We got into a fight."

I turned to face her. "You two didn't break up, did you?"

It was strange that I cared. I usually tired of my mother's boyfriends long before she did.

She shrugged. "Who knows? Who cares?" She turned away and began straightening up my bed. "I've learned that nothing in life is permanent."

My mother was not a good actress. She couldn't fool me. I saw moisture gathering in her eyes before she could turn away from me. I knew she cared about Chuck more than she would ever admit.

"You're wrong, Mom," I said. "Some things are permanent—like love and peace, for example. Even relationships, if you let them be."

"Then why is Neil dead right now?" She unconsciously beat my pillow into shape with angry fists.

"Neil's body is dead. His soul is alive."

"They're teaching you strange philosophies at that church. That's exactly what started the argument between me and Chuck, if you can believe it—you and your crazy church. Chuck thinks this whole thing is terrific."

"And what do you think?"

"You *know* what I think. Look—I'll be the first to admit that it's been good for you, but I also know religion is a—"

"Not religion," I interrupted. "Jesus."

"Jesus, then, is a crutch," she went on. "As soon as you're over Neil, you'll be over Jesus."

The doorbell rang.

"Don't be so sure," I warned, brushing past her.

I threw open the door and there stood Grady. He was dressed for the occasion: straw hat, checkered shirt, overalls, old boots—the works. He looked great!

"My prince!" I cried.

He came in and exchanged formalities with Mom. She did nothing to make him feel welcome, but it didn't seem to faze him. She followed us out the door.

"I need to go to the store," she explained. "Have a good time tonight."

As we walked to Grady's car, we listened to her attempt to start the engine. It refused to turn over.

"Let's go see what the trouble is," Grady offered.

I sighed and followed him back up the drive. Opening the hood, he tinkered with the engine and then slammed it down.

"It looks like you're overdue for a tune-up," he said. "I can do it for you."

"Would you?" My mother seemed pleased. "My car has been doing this for the last week. I was going to ask Chuck about it, but he might not be around for a while to fix it."

"I can do it tomorrow."

"Okay. Thanks."

"Can we stop at the store for you?" Grady asked.

"Oh, no, that won't be necessary," Mom said, climbing out of the car. "I can go tomorrow. Thanks anyway."

*I think Grady just got on Mom's good side.* Grady could definitely win the respect and approval of the people he came into contact with.

As Grady's Chevy moved slowly over the gravel road toward the barn, we saw at least ten people already standing around. I eyed the two brown horses tied to the wagon nearby. They pawed the ground nervously and seemed eager to get going.

"It looks like you have as many as you can carry on this cart," said an old man leaning against the wagon.

I watched him lead the horses out of the barn and check to see if they were cinched up properly. Removing his hat to scratch behind his ears, he said to us, "I'll send the rest out on another wagon. Go ahead and get on this one."

Laughing and chattering, everyone climbed up the sides of the wagon and plunged into the rough straw. As I settled myself beside Grady at the rear, the wagon began to sway from side to side. I found myself being repeatedly thrown against him. Grady pulled me over closer and leaned back against the sideboard, his arm around my shoulder. I stiffened and remained upright.

"Would you please relax, Andrea?" Grady whispered gently into my ear. "Let's be friends. I'm not going to hurt you. I promise."

I laid my head back against his arm and tried to relax.

What was I so afraid of? The country air smelled fresh and I inhaled deeply. Closing my eyes, I imagined that Neil's strong arms were around me. As the dream became believable, it became easier to relax. Soon, Neil would kiss me. . . .

As I listened to the rotating of the wagon wheels and the clip-clop of the horses' hooves, I realized this evening would be entirely different than I'd anticipated. If Neil had been here, he'd have stirred up a little excitement. He would have set off firecrackers to scare the horses or turned the wagon over and buried someone in the hay.

I didn't have to worry about anything like that with this group. Surprisingly enough, I found myself glad that it wouldn't be a wild time. I knew it wasn't that these kids weren't capable of instigating something. I'd heard them talk about all the crazy things they'd done together, but they weren't destructive when they had fun.

Tonight was for couples. Seated around the wagon, they talked quietly and held hands. At least for tonight, I was part of a couple. I could feel secure.

At least for tonight, I didn't have to worry about Cheryl Riley.

At least for tonight, I felt special to someone.

I wanted this evening to last forever.

# 10

"Is your mother out with Chuck tonight?" Grady asked as we drove home.

"No. They had a fight."

"That's too bad. What's she doing?"

"Probably sitting at home crying or watching TV. She could be out with another guy, for all I know."

"Let's go see."

"What for?"

"I'd like to get to know her a little better, that's all."

"You would? Neil never cared about my mother."

"I'm not Neil."

"Of course you aren't. I was just thinking out loud."

I was right about my mother. When we walked in the front door, she was clutching a handkerchief in one hand and staring morosely at the television. Her eyes looked slightly puffy. She sniffed as she rose from the couch.

"Oh, hello. If you'll excuse me, I was just going to bed."

"Hey, it's still early." Grady placed his hand on her arm. He was so warm and gentle. He was always touching people, giving them special recognition. "Why don't we pop some popcorn and play a game of Monopoly?"

"Monopoly?" My mother wrinkled her nose, then looked thoughtful. "Yeah, that might be fun for a change."

"I'm not sure we still have the game," I said as I began poking around in the hall closet. Neil and I had never played games.

I finally found the Monopoly game in the back of the closet under a pile of *National Geographic* magazines. Tucking it under one arm, I entered the kitchen to find Grady emptying the popcorn popper into a bowl and my mother pouring apple juice into glasses.

*What a cozy evening,* I thought as we began battling over the most sought-after property deeds.

My mother, in spite of her obvious attempts to remain aloof, seemed to be talking and laughing more easily as the evening progressed. As usual, much of the conversation revolved around Neil.

"I suppose your family's religion is what helped you cope with Neil's death," Mom said at one point.

Grady nodded. "Yeah, it's still tough, especially on weekends and when we're sitting down to dinner—times when Neil might have been with us." He paused. "Without God we would have come completely unglued."

"I don't spend much time thinking about religion," she said just as she landed on Marvin Gardens and began to count out the $850 she owed me. I gladly stuffed the needed money under my side of the board. "It seems to have helped Andrea through this time."

Recently, Mother hadn't said anything about my going to church so much, and she hadn't mentioned Aunt Martha again. Maybe Chuck had convinced her that Christians weren't crazy after all. She never took me very seriously, but I knew she listened to Chuck.

The clock on the mantel chimed twelve-thirty. In my efforts to come from behind in the game, I hadn't realized that so much time had passed.

"I think I'll go to bed now." My mother faked a yawn.

She assumed Grady and I wanted to be alone.

I was nearly certain Grady didn't share Neil's passion for getting me alone in the dark at the end of our dates. He wouldn't attack me the minute my mother left the room.

Grady proved me right.

"Yeah, I gotta be going," Grady said.

"You're welcome to stay . . ." Mom began.

"Thank you, but I want to get over here early tomorrow to work on your car. I've really enjoyed the evening."

Grady took my hand in his as we walked to the door.

"As Neil always said, 'You're really all right.'" He smiled and closed the door softly behind him, leaving me to wonder just exactly what he meant.

The expression "all right" to Neil had meant comfortable, just right, something that perfectly fit. Is that what Grady was saying also?

"I thought you two might want to be alone," Mom said as she opened the dishwasher and began to methodically load it with dishes.

"We're just good friends, Mom."

"So far," she added. "He seems nice. l guess I have to get to know him better."

"Yeah. He doesn't talk as much as Neil," I added.

Grady was different than Neil in some ways, but similar to him in others. Neil's spirit seemed to live on in Grady. When Grady laughed, I heard Neil. When Grady squeezed my hand, it rekindled emotions in me that I thought had died with Neil.

Grady, of course, had no idea how I felt. As far as I could tell, he and Cheryl remained a cozy pair. Why should that bother me so intensely? Suddenly, to be Grady's friend simply wasn't enough. I wanted more from him, but I didn't know exactly what.

"All I know is that I like being with Grady," I said aloud as I rinsed off the last plate, handed it to my mother, and left the room. "More than I like being with anyone else."

I had just stepped out of the shower on Saturday morning when I heard the doorbell. Grady was here already. I'd never known Neil to be early for anything.

I pulled on a pair of jeans and a T-shirt and ran back to the bathroom to dry my hair. I hated this rushing around. If Grady was the prompt type, I would have to think about getting more organized myself.

I took one last look at myself in the full-length mirror on my closet door and ran outside to find Grady bent over the engine of Mom's car. It was a familiar sight. Neil had been forever working on engines, taking them apart and putting them back together. It had always reminded me of a child with a Tinkertoy set.

Neil's cap, perched perfectly on Grady's head, created the full effect. He straightened up when he heard me clear my throat. "Hi." His eyes looked admiringly at me. "You look pretty today."

I was glad he found me attractive.

"Thank you." I peered under the hood, the maze of metal parts meaning nothing to me. "How's it coming?"

"I'll have it done in a little while. Would you like to go for a ride later?"

"Sure. It's so nice of you to do this for my mother."

"I have a soft heart when it comes to cars. I can't stand to see them sick."

"That's the way Neil felt about bikes," I hesitated.

Now was as good a time as any to ask a question that had often troubled me. "Was Neil really into dope—like you said?"

"Forget I ever brought it up, Andrea. It doesn't matter now, does it?"

"It matters a lot. I don't like to think he lied to me."

"Okay." He leaned against the car and crossed his arms in front of his chest. "I'm going to tell you this once, and then we won't need to talk about it again. He shot speed while he was at school. He claimed it helped him study better. He dropped acid a few times too. Some of his friends were dopers. They probably pressured him."

"But Neil was a leader," I protested. "He could have said no. Why woudn't he tell me? Why would he lie?"

"He probably figured there was no reason to tell you. He loved you and he didn't want to lose you." He paused and changed position. "Hey, Neil wasn't perfect, but to call him a liar is way too harsh. When it was easier, he avoided the truth, that's all. It was just one of his problems. Don't think less of him. We all have problems, Andrea. The difference with us is that we have God to help us overcome them, but Neil didn't—not until it was too late."

*If Neil had a lying problem, then he was possibly just bragging when he told Grady about shooting speed,* I thought to myself.

"Did Neil tell you he loved me?" I asked.

"Yeah. Lots of times. If he wouldn't have told me, I'd have known anyway. When a guy's in love, it's obvious."

"Have you ever been in love, Grady?" I asked.

"Me?" He chuckled softly. "You're putting me on the spot."

"That's true. It's none of my business."

He became serious. "That's what I like about you. You're up front. I can understand how Neil fell in love with you." He ducked his head under the hood and resumed his tinkering. "I'll never get done here if you keep distracting me with these questions."

"Does that mean you're not going to tell me if you've ever been in love?" I persisted.

He laughed. "Just for the record, I don't think I've ever been in love. But if loving a girl is anything like loving Jesus, it must be great."

Mom appeared then carrying two glasses of lemonade. "Drew Bradshaw called while you were in the shower. He said he'd call back later." She placed a hand on Grady's shoulder. "Is everything okay under there?"

"It'll run like a new Cadillac by the time I get done," he joked.

"Wonderful. As long as it continues to get the gas mileage of a Ford."

"Have you been dating Drew?" Grady asked when Mom had gone back into the house.

"I run into him sometimes, but we haven't dated. I don't feel much like dating at this point. I'm lonely without Neil, but I'm not sure about dating anyone else."

"Why not? Wouldn't Neil want you to go on living?"

"Living is different than dating," I answered. "Your loyalty to Neil will always stay intact because you'll never have another brother. If I start dating, it's almost as though I'd be looking for someone to take his place."

"What about the Dayspring concert and the hayride? Weren't those dates?"

"Not really. You admitted yourself that you took me to the concert because you wanted me to meet Jesus. The hayride, well, Cheryl is out of town and I just figured—"

Grady slammed the hood down, giving me his full attention. "I didn't ask you to the concert just because I wanted you to become a Christian. That was part of it. It is true that if you'd rejected Christ, I might not be seeing you as often as I am now." He paused, then went on in a rush of words. "Now I find myself trying to get too close to you. Not that it matters. Your loyalty to Neil is like a protective wall you've built around yourself. And you're not letting me or anyone else in."

I couldn't believe what I was hearing. Grady wanted in closer—past my wall. What wall?

"I don't know what you're talking about."

"I know you loved Neil," Grady said, speaking more gently. "I'm not putting that down, but he's gone and he's not coming back. You can't go on living like nothing has changed. The course of your life has been altered. Can't you accept that?"

"No!" I shouted angrily.

Grady didn't understand. He'd never been in love. Even though he too missed Neil, he couldn't understand the intense longing in my heart to be with his brother again. What I wouldn't give to feel Neil's strong arms around me, holding me again.

Involuntarily the tears began streaming down my cheeks. Grady held out his hand. "I'm sorry, Andrea. You're right. I don't understand about you and Neil. I'll try, if you'll just let me into a tiny corner of your heart."

"You already have a corner," I sobbed, taking his hand. "But I don't know what Neil would think—"

"That doesn't matter anymore," Grady cut in. "What's important now is what you think—what I think."

His hand was warm and firm, and for his sake, I tried to respond positively. But I couldn't. All I could think about was how different his hand felt than Neil's.

Watching my face, Grady said, "I'm in no hurry. I'm willing to give you all the time you need."

The front door slammed and Grady turned back to the car.

"Are you all done?" my mother asked as she came around the corner.

Grady nodded. "It should run good now." He knelt down and began gathering up his tools.

She pulled her wallet out of her purse. "Is twenty dollars enough?"

"I don't want to be paid."

"Oh, but I would have paid a mechanic. Let me pay you for the parts."

Grady put up his hands. "I get parts for practically nothing at Ed's, where I work. I enjoy working on cars. Honest."

Mom shook her head. "Even Chuck would have charged

me for the parts. Thanks a lot."

"Is it okay if I take Andrea out to lunch and for a ride this afternoon? We'll be home by four o'clock."

"Sure. That will be fine."

She looked a little surprised. It was apparent that she didn't know quite how to take Grady.

Neil had never thought it was necessary to inform my mother either of where we were going or the time we planned to return. It wasn't that he had meant to be inconsiderate. He just hadn't liked being limited.

Grady took me to a cute little French cafe in another part of town. We shared a sandwich at a table outside. After lunch we went for a long ride in the country. We stopped once to pick wild strawberries by the side of the road and again to pet some horses.

Grady couldn't pass a garage-sale sign without stopping. It was fun. Neil had never bothered with garage sales. It was just someone else's junk as far as he was concerned.

Grady bought a birdcage for a friend, a couple of old tools for his dad, and a watch for his mother. When I admired a crystal vase, he bought it for me.

We returned home at four o'clock like he had promised. I was pleasantly surprised to see Chuck's station wagon parked in the driveway.

"I want you to meet Chuck," I said as Grady parked in the driveway behind Chuck's car.

"Okay, but I can only stay for a few minutes," Grady told me. "I don't want your mother to think I'm trying to move in."

"She doesn't think much about what my friends and I do. Sometimes I wish she did."

When we entered the house, I saw nothing unusual. Chuck sat in the living room watching TV and Mom banged around in the kitchen. It smelled like she was cooking dinner.

I introduced Chuck and Grady to each other. My mother insisted Grady stay for dinner.

"I'd better not," Grady started to refuse. "Andrea's probably sick of me."

"Don't be silly." I punched him in the arm. "I've put up with you this long. What's a couple more hours?"

Grady gave in and asked if he could call his mother to tell her his plans. It always surprised me when Grady did things like that. I was so used to doing whatever I pleased with no concern for anyone else. Watching Grady was fast becoming a lesson in unselfishness and consideration.

Dinner couldn't have been more pleasant. Grady complimented Mom on the food until she blushed with embarrassment. He seemed to hit it off instantly with Chuck. For some reason it was very important to me that they like each other.

After dinner, Grady and I rode along with Chuck and my mom to look at an old '65 Chevy that Chuck was interested in buying. I soon found that when it came to cars, Chuck and Grady could talk nonstop. Chuck liked the Chevy, and when Grady offered to help him restore it, he said he appreciated the offer and would seriously consider it.

"I need to be going now," Grady said when we'd returned home and Chuck and my mom had gone into the house. "It's been a good day. I feel like that wall of yours is beginning to crumble. Maybe together we can build something better," Grady said as he looked into my face.

"I can't think of anyone now that I'd rather try with," I smiled.

"We might have to put our building plans on hold for a while," Grady began. "I'm leaving for Canada next weekend with my parents. We'll be gone for about three weeks." He paused. "I wondered if—would you like to come to dinner at my house next Friday night?"

I swallowed. "Dinner—with your parents there and everything?"

He laughed. "They usually do put in an appearance at the dinner table."

"I'd rather not. They don't like me—"

"They don't really know you," Grady interrupted. "You never let them get to know you."

"They have formed definite opinions about me, and I know they're not positive ones. Whose idea was this dinner, anyway?" I asked.

"It doesn't matter whose idea it was," Grady answered. "Look, it's no big deal. We'll just eat with them and then we'll find something else to do."

I disagreed. It *was* a big deal.

Wanting to please Grady, I told him I'd come. Somehow we'd suffer through it together. How would they handle sitting across the table making conversation with the one they felt was responsible for leading their oldest son astray?

# 11

$\mathcal{I}$ looked forward to Sundays, not only because I'd see Grady, but because I was excited to learn more about my new life.

I had learned many of the worship songs by heart, and I was becoming more familiar with my Bible. When Pastor Thorsen asked us to look up certain verses, it was becoming easier for me to find them.

This particular Sunday, when I walked into the sanctuary I suddenly felt like turning around and going out the way I had come in.

Grady and his parents sat in the third row from the front. Cheryl Riley occupied the seat beside Grady. She was as close as she could be without sitting on his lap.

After spending the weekend with Grady and after all the personal feelings we'd shared, it seemed cruel for him to flaunt his relationship with Cheryl.

I found a seat in the opposite aisle to the rear of where they sat. It seemed like a waste of time to stay in church that Sunday. My eyes refused to focus on anything but Grady and Cheryl. I watched her whisper into his ear. He would respond by smiling or leaning over and whispering back. They sure looked at each other a lot.

Maybe yesterday I had read more into Grady's words than what he'd really meant to say. Maybe he threw out personal statements like that all the time and didn't expect anyone to take him seriously.

I left before Pastor Thorsen had concluded his message.

I didn't see Grady until Wednesday when he came into Tebo's for lunch. He reminded me of my promise to come to dinner.

During the next two days I kept wanting to call to tell him I couldn't make it. Whenever I saw the Hollingers at church, they still treated me coldly—at least Mrs. Hollinger did. Grady's dad was at least cordial.

How would we spend an entire evening together?

I knew that if I backed out, Grady would ask Cheryl to come instead. Thinking about that was even worse than spending an uncomfortable evening with his family.

Grady offered to pick me up and bring me to his house that evening, but I told him I'd drive over.

I changed my clothes on Friday afternoon four times before I finally decided to wear my black dress with tiny white flowers on it. I was glad my mother wasn't home to see me try on one dress after the other.

Mom and I had grown steadily closer in the weeks since Neil's death. We still never talked about anything real deep. As always, she steered the conversation aside whenever it got heavy, but at least we were communicating. That was more than we'd done before.

Hearing a motorcycle pull up, I ran to the front window and saw Drew walking up the driveway. He always seemed to show up at the most inopportune times.

I had to admit I was kind of attracted to him. He was not only handsome, but he had a way of drawing me in with his eyes that made me wonder what it would be like to go out with him.

"Hi," he greeted when I opened the door. "Where are you going all dolled up?"

"The Hollingers' for dinner," I returned.

"Oh." He looked disappointed. "The summer is flying

by and you haven't given me one date yet. What would Neil think?"

*Good question,* I thought.

"It looks like tonight's out," Drew muttered. "I don't like to plan so far in advance, but how about next Friday? We can go out to dinner and then go to the bike races at Delta."

If he had suggested anything other than the bike races, I might not have been interested. I didn't feel like I knew Drew well enough to risk an entire evening of possible boredom or intimidation, but I loved cycle races. Most of our crowd were bike enthusiasts. They would certainly be at the races, and that meant I wouldn't be spending the whole time alone with Drew.

"Well, what do you say?" he asked impatiently.

"Next Friday night would be fine."

He looked surprised. "It would?" He grinned. "Great. I'll pick you up at six o'clock."

He hurried away, probably wanting to get away before I changed my mind. I wasn't sure I'd made the right decision, but he was gone and I couldn't change my mind.

I waited until the last possible moment to leave for the Hollingers'. This was my opportunity to make a good impression, and I didn't want to blow it by being late. I had to prove I was good enough for a Hollinger. All I could do was be myself and hope for the best.

Grady met me at the door. He was wearing a pair of jeans and a blue sweater. One thing about Grady and Neil—when they weren't working on engines, they were always clean.

Grady looked like he'd just stepped out of the shower, his hair still damp.

Neil had not been quite so meticulous about his appearance. He never really cared about clothes and stayed a safe distance from a barber's chair. Only when he could no longer see because of the hair covering his eyes did he consent to get it cut.

What I wouldn't give to be standing in front of Neil now instead of his little brother.

Even the Hollingers couldn't intimidate me when Neil was around. He had been so protective. With Grady, I didn't feel secure. I knew he cared about me, but his allegiance to his parents was very evident. If the situation got out of hand, I couldn't be sure Grady would stand by me.

"Hi." Grady's smile produced in me the calming effect he probably intended to give. I relaxed a little. He led me into the kitchen where his mother was dropping carrots into a pot on the stove.

"Hello, Andrea." She glanced in our direction before she turned back to the stove. "Grady mentioned that you would be joining us this evening. We're so pleased you could come."

*Who is she trying to kid?*

"It's so nice of you to have me," I replied awkwardly.

"Did Grady tell you we're leaving for Canada on Sunday?" She began dicing potatoes now in neat little cubes. Not waiting for me to answer, she continued. "We'll be gone three weeks. I wish it could be longer, but Ken can't get away from the plant."

Mr. Hollinger entered the kitchen. Crossing the room in long strides, he stopped beside Grady.

"Well, hello, Andrea." His eyes sparkled with life. "It's been a while since we've seen you around here. Just because Neil's gone doesn't mean you're not welcome here. Right, Marilyn?"

He actually said that as if he meant it. Maybe I'd stuck the wrong label on him all this time. Maybe he thought I was okay.

When Mrs. Hollinger didn't answer, I felt my cheeks grow warm.

"Isn't that right, Marilyn?" Mr. Hollinger repeated. "Andrea's always welcome here, isn't she?"

"Of course, Ken, of course," Mrs. Hollinger said brusquely. "Grady, why don't you take Andrea down to the game room? I'll call you when dinner's ready."

"Sure, Mom."

I followed Grady down to the basement. After putting on a CD, he opened the refrigerator and pulled out two cans of Coke. "Don't let Mom make you nervous, Andrea. She can't talk and cook at the same time, that's all."

It seemed to me that those two activities could be done together with little or no problem. I often used to stand in the kitchen and talk to my mom while she cooked dinner.

Grady and I played Ping-Pong until his mother called us twenty minutes later.

"Can I help you with anything?" I asked as I entered the kitchen.

"Everything is on the table," she answered coolly. "Just sit down over there," she said, pointing to a chair.

I mentally kicked myself for not asking to help sooner. When Cheryl came for dinner, they probably worked together in the kitchen.

The conversation during the first ten minutes of the meal consisted of "Please pass the meat loaf, the potatoes, the carrots, the biscuits . . ." Following came, "How's your mother, summer, car?"

*So far so good. Keep it light, crack a joke or two,* I reminded myself. *We're staying on top.*

"The meat loaf is delicious," I complimented as I took a second helping.

"Thank you, Andrea," she answered. "I was beginning to wonder. Nobody said anything."

"Marilyn, you know what we think of your cooking," Mr. Hollinger said. "Forgive us."

"It's good, Mom," Grady added. "I love the biscuits."

"Thank you, dear. Which reminds me, I've got to get this bun warmer back to Ruth. She might need it while we're gone. You'll be seeing Cheryl tomorrow night, won't you? You can take it with you when you go to pick her up."

I looked up from my food and caught Grady staring uneasily at me. He turned his attention quickly back to his mother.

"Sure, Mom."

Me one night, Cheryl the next. His mother had purposely mentioned Grady's plans for the following evening. She wanted to make sure I knew that someone else held the number one spot in her son's heart and life.

I hardly tasted the rest of my dinner. I didn't even understand why it should bother me. Of course he would want to spend his last night with Cheryl.

Neil would never have done something like that. I never worried that he was dating any of those beautiful college co-eds. He knew how to make me feel absolutely secure.

"Andrea, you're the only girl I'll ever love," he had often assured me.

I had always known where I stood with Neil. How could I expect more out of Grady than he was already giving? He was only being kind in trying to fill the big hole in my heart. There was nothing serious between us.

"We were so pleased to hear that you've given your heart to the Lord." Mrs. Hollinger removed the cloth napkin from her lap and placed it neatly on the table, then pushed her plate away. "Do you find it's made a difference in your life?"

"Yeah, I find that I think a little differently now. Things that used to seem so important don't matter so much anymore."

"Wonderful," Mrs. Hollinger said. "The Bible tells us to be renewed in the spirit of our minds."

"Grady says you see Drew Bradshaw sometimes," said

Mr. Hollinger. "He hasn't been around since the funeral. How's he doing?"

"No need to worry about him," Grady remarked. "Drew can take care of himself."

"He seems to be doing okay," I said. "I really don't know him that well."

"He's working to change that," Grady mumbled.

I smiled. He talked as though it bothered him that Drew was interested in me.

During dinner the conversation never included Neil. We didn't discuss anything that really mattered. We just made small talk.

Mrs. Hollinger jumped up and began clearing the table at the first lull. I followed suit, but after bumping into her twice on our many trips back and forth to the kitchen, I began to feel as though I was in the way. Instead, I decided to load the dishwasher.

"I probably won't be needing a dishwasher much longer," Mrs. Hollinger remarked as she stepped to my side and rearranged all the bowls I had so neatly positioned. "Soon Grady will be away at college. Like Neil, he'll be going to State. Cheryl Riley's parents are sending her there also. Have you met Grady's girlfriend, Andrea?"

I nodded.

"She's nice. You ought to get to know her. She's been a Christian since she was little. I remember the day Cheryl accepted Christ. It was so sweet. We've known the Rileys for years. How many years have we known the Rileys, Grady?"

Grady, who stood at the sink rinsing a plate, looked very uncomfortable. Although my jealousy of Cheryl remained intact, I almost felt sorry for him.

He shrugged. "Ten years, maybe."

"It's been longer than that. You were just a toddler when they moved across the street."

She placed the last glass in the dishwasher and closed the door. I'd had all I could take of the wonderful Cheryl Riley.

"I hate to do this, Andrea," Mrs. Hollinger said as she hung her apron carefully on a hook under the sink. "But tonight is the only time I have to prepare my Sunday school lesson. Will you excuse me?"

My attempt to appear disappointed probably wasn't very convincing. "Of course," I said happily. "I understand."

When she had left the room, Grady caught my eye and motioned for me to follow him. We traveled through the living room where his dad was watching TV and down a long hallway to the room at the end—Neil's bedroom. He threw the door open and flipped on the light. I noticed in an instant the motorcycle posters, my photograph on Neil's desk, the seldom-worn helmet on the floor by his bed, and a hundred other familiar objects. The memory of Neil resurrected once again.

I began to feel choked up inside as I picked up one of his medical books and leafed through it. At his parents' insistence, Neil had been pursuing a medical career. I would have been really surprised if he had finished even his second year. Neil hadn't taken school very seriously.

I picked up a small bunch of snapshots lying on his desk: Neil and Drew in their dorm room; Neil on his bike; Neil and I at the beach; Neil and Drew at what looked like a party—then I stopped. The next two snapshots were of Neil and a girl—one with his arm around her, and the other, holding her on his lap.

As hard as I tried, I couldn't see anything in either one of their expressions to reveal what kind of a relationship they had shared.

She was very pretty, with long blond hair and big, beautiful blue eyes. I wanted to think the pictures had been taken before we'd started dating. But Neil's hair was too long, so they had to be recent snaps. It was apparent that they had come from the same roll of film as the picture of Neil and me.

Neil loved to party, I reasoned, and must have gone to many parties at school without me. There was nothing wrong with that. Of course girls showed up at the parties all the time. . . .

"Don't let those bother you." Grady rose from Neil's bed where he'd been sitting quietly all this time. He took the photos from me, opened a desk drawer and shoved them in. "Neil was popular. He had lots of friends."

"We're going to start cleaning in here soon. I want you to look around and choose what you'd like to have."

"Oh, Grady, you mean it?"

He nodded.

I studied the room carefully. Was there anything that I *didn't* want? I wished I could scoop it all up and haul it home. I wondered if taking it all home would help. Neil's things could never take the place of Neil himself.

And then I saw it—the giant stuffed teddy bear.

The memory of the day he won it suddenly rushed back. We'd already walked around the state fair for hours when Neil stopped at a booth and began bouncing dimes off the glass plates. We laughed together and our cheers rose as coin after coin landed on the plate and then bounced off.

After wasting eight dollars, it wasn't funny anymore, and I sensed Neil's impatience. He was drunk, and his judgment was bad. Too often his dimes missed the plates altogether.

"Let me try, Neil, let me try," I pleaded.

He chuckled, but handed me three dimes. My third dime landed in the middle of the plate, rolled precariously around the edge, then back toward the center where it stopped, winning me the giant red teddy bear.

Neil never heard the end of it. We'd lugged it into the house to show Grady, and I'd forgotten to take it home. It was no wonder that I forgot it, because it was that night for the first time that Neil told me he loved me as we sat in the gazebo in his backyard. Who could think about teddy bears at a time like that?

Now I coveted that stuffed bear. It would be an ever-present reminder of Neil's love.

"I'd like that teddy bear, Grady." I pointed to it.

Grady placed it in my arms. "He's all yours. What else?"

As I was scanning the room again, Mrs. Hollinger appeared in the doorway. She frowned fiercely.

"What's going on in here?" she demanded.

"We're just—I was letting Andrea choose something of Neil's to take home," Grady explained. "You don't mind, do you? We were going to clean the room soon anyway."

"Yes, but we haven't yet," she snapped. "I haven't decided what I'm going to do with Neil's belongings. Until I do, I want everything to remain exactly as Neil left it." She turned her attention to me. "I'm sorry, Andrea. I hope you'll—"

"Mom, that's silly!" Grady interrupted. "Something has to be done with this stuff. Why not give it to those who loved Neil the most?"

"I'll decide who loved him the most." Mrs. Hollinger's voice rose sharply. "We'll discuss this later, Grady."

"I'm sorry, Mrs. Hollinger," I began. "I had no idea—"

"Think nothing about it," she cut me off. "Now—I'm sure there's a better room in which to entertain your friends, Grady."

I didn't want to be entertained anymore. I couldn't wait to get out of there.

"I'd better be going," I told Grady as soon as she was gone. I stepped quickly across the room and set the teddy bear in its former resting place in the corner.

"It's only eight o'clock." His gaze refused to meet mine. "I'm sorry about Mom, Andrea. She's just super-sensitive these days. It's my fault. I should have asked her—"

I shook my head. "She can't stand me, Grady. It's written all over her face. Why she would even agree to this dinner is beyond me."

Grady was silent for a moment. "Maybe I'm trying too hard. It's just so important to me that the two of you reach some kind of understanding. Maybe it would be better if I laid off and let her do it on her own."

"There was a time when I used to get an icy stare from your dad. He at least seems to have mellowed."

"My dad and I are pretty close. We've done a lot of talking in the last few weeks since Neil died. He's softened up a lot. Mom's keeping too much of it inside." He took my hand. "I told Marc and Jill we might drop by tonight. Let's go over there and try to relax and forget this ever happened."

We passed Grady's mother at her desk in the dining room on our way out. Her head resting on her hands, she looked up at us with tired eyes.

"Thank you for dinner," I said.

"You're welcome. You're not going anywhere, are you, Grady?"

"We're going over to Jill's."

"You've got a busy schedule tomorrow."

"I won't be late," he said as he pulled me toward the door.

"What? Leaving so soon?" Mr. Hollinger called from the living room. "Come back when you can stay longer, Andrea."

"Thank you," I said and Grady whisked me out the door.

The night air felt cool and crisp as we climbed into Grady's car. The coolness of the summer evening became warmth compared to the cold freeze emitted from Grady's mother.

We joined Marc and Jill by the swimming pool in the Wagners' backyard. I found it difficult to join in the conversation. I'd allowed Grady's mom to totally dampen things, so an hour later when Grady suggested we go, I didn't protest.

We didn't talk much on the way back. Grady parked his Chevy in the driveway and walked me to my car.

"I'm going to miss you," he said softly as we stood together in the darkness.

Would he be repeating that same phrase to Cheryl tomorrow night?

"I almost wish I weren't going," he went on. "But Mom needs the rest. She's a wreck."

A moment of silence followed; then our eyes met. Grady drew me close to him, then suddenly the Hollingers' porch light flashed on and we quickly drew apart. Grady smiled helplessly. His lips brushed my cheek as he whispered, "I'll call you as soon as I get back."

And then he disappeared into the darkness.

I wanted desperately to believe him, but I couldn't. I knew his mother would do everything in her power to stop our relationship from progressing any further.

# 12

*I* thought I'd see Grady at church on Sunday morning; instead, the Rileys occupied the Hollingers' usual row in the front of the church. Apparently, Grady and his family had already left for Canada.

Instead of concentrating and involving myself in the church service, I sat wondering what Grady and Cheryl had done last night. What had they talked about?

It would be three long weeks before I would see Grady again. And even when he did come home, I didn't know if we would share anything more than friendship based on our mutual love for Neil. I wanted to believe that the things he talked to me about were really from his heart.

Grady made me mad! I had never gone through this with Neil. We'd loved each other from the very beginning. We'd given all of ourselves to each other, and there was never a question about how we felt.

Grady was much more cautious than Neil. I should have been thankful for that, because I wasn't sure I trusted myself to keep my feelings under control if I would ever consider anyone else. With Neil, when I had let myself go, my love for him couldn't be stopped. I didn't even try to hold it in. I had had no regrets about my relationship with Neil, but now that I was a Christian I felt like I needed to be more careful.

What exactly was going on inside of me at the thought of seeing Grady's handsome face or hearing the sound of his deep voice?

Suddenly I realized that the service was over and the sanctuary emptying.

As the congregation streamed by toward the exit, one pair of eyes singled me out. As our eyes met, Cheryl shot me an icy stare. I glanced away quickly and headed toward the side door.

I knew Cheryl's feelings for me were less than friendly, but usually we just acted indifferent toward each other. It had never been expressed as outward contempt.

Without warning, tears sprang to my eyes. Neil was gone. Grady was gone. I had just received a hateful look at a place where I expected to find love and acceptance. Heading for the door, I unexpectedly ran into Jill. She grabbed my arm and held me from going any farther.

"Where are you going in such a hurry?" She searched my face. "Hey, what's the matter?"

"Nothing," I lied.

Jill stared at me uncomfortably. "That's a pretty dress," she said. "The youth group is going out for brunch. Want to come?"

"I can't. I'll—see you later."

I could feel Jill watching my every step as I headed for my car. Once inside, I released the pent-up emotion within me. "Why couldn't I have died with Neil?" I sobbed. "What is this, God, some kind of punishment? I thought living for you was going to be the answer to all my problems. But no, it's just created a whole new set. I've lost all my friends—"

Suddenly the passenger door flew open and Jill climbed in beside me. Without asking any questions, she placed a gentle hand on my shoulder and began to pray.

"Thanks," I mumbled when I'd finally stopped crying.

"Is it Neil?" she asked.

"What else is there?"

"Andrea . . ." Jill began, then stopped as if searching for the right words. "You can find a new life without him. It's entirely up to you, but I'm not sure you even really want to try."

"What do you mean?"

Jill took a deep breath. "You've got to let Jesus be to you everything that Neil can't be. The Holy Spirit wants to be your comforter, but you're not letting Him." She hesitated. "Sooner or later you're going to have to let go of Neil."

"Let go of him?" I looked at her incredulously and realized that, like all the others, she didn't get it. "Jill, you still have Marc to love you. You'll probably marry him someday. How can you possibly understand?"

"I don't claim to understand. I do want to help you, though, and I refuse to sit back and watch you be destroyed by—by your refusing to let go of the past. You have too much to live for."

I tensely gripped the steering wheel. "I appreciate your wanting to help, but there's really not a thing you or anyone else can do, is there?"

"No—not as long as you hold on to the past—and Neil Hollinger."

Nothing else was said. A moment later I watched Jill, hand in hand with Marc, cross the parking lot and climb into a car with a group of laughing, carefree kids on their way to brunch. Neil was gone, yet for everyone except me life continued as always.

My relationship with Jill seemed strained during the following week. She acted as friendly as ever, and even invited me to join her and Marc for lunch every day. I always refused, not able to forgive her for asking me to let go of Neil. It wasn't even an option, because if I had to let go of Neil, I didn't even know how to go about it.

I wondered why I missed Grady so much. In hopes that he'd at least write me a postcard, I hurried home each day of that first week to see if I'd received any mail. I was disappointed every time. He was probably having too much fun to be thinking about me. I wondered if he was writing to Cheryl. I wished I could peek into her mailbox!

Wanting to avoid contact with Cheryl, I skipped youth group that week. By the time Friday rolled around, I was so bored and restless that my evening with Drew was a welcome distraction. I determined not to bore Drew by talking too much about Neil *or* Jesus. Neil had probably told Drew all about me, and it was important that I be the person he'd described. Drew would wonder what Neil ever saw in me if I seemed different than that. I'd prove to Drew that Neil had had good taste.

When the doorbell rang, I took a quick peek in the mirror to make sure everything looked okay before I answered the door.

"Hey, you look gorgeous." Drew grinned as his eyes moved approvingly from my face to my green cashmere sweater.

I followed Drew to the silver van parked at the curb. *The Bradshaw family must really have money,* I thought as he helped me into the van.

Neil's family was quite wealthy too, but you'd never have known it to look at Neil. Materialism turned him off, and he never took advantage of his parents' money.

"Am I dreaming?" Drew remarked as he maneuvered the van onto the freeway. "Are we really out on a date together? I was about ready to give up."

"It was the only way I could get you off my back," I teased. "You're such a pest."

"I'll bet you didn't make Neil wait this long for a date."

"No—but that was different. Our relationship was meant to be from the very start."

"And we're not?"

I shrugged. "Who knows? I sure can't predict the future. I thought Neil and I would be together forever."

"Tell me about you and Neil," Drew urged. "He sure talked a lot about you."

"It was incredible," I started.

Out spilled many highlights of the last year, and with it my resolve not to bore Drew talking too much about Neil.

When we finally pulled into the parking lot of a fancy Chinese restaurant outside of town, I took a deep breath.

"I'm sorry, Drew," I apologized. "I don't think I've stopped talking since we left my house."

"That's okay." He turned off the ignition and sat still for a moment. "You needed to do that. Don't you feel better now?"

I had to admit that I did.

While we waited for our order, Drew talked and I listened. Then together we discussed the Trailblazers, Neil's favorite basketball team. We talked about his favorite rock groups, foods, and subjects in school.

"What's your favorite Chinese food?" Drew asked.

"Neil loved egg foo yung."

"Not Neil's favorite—yours."

I hesitated. "Well, I like egg foo yung too."

"Why?"

"Because it's what Neil liked—oh, I don't know," I finished lamely.

After dinner we headed toward a little town called Astor, where the bike races were being held. I'd gone the previous summer with Neil.

As we walked toward the bleachers, I looked up to see a small group of people flailing their arms at us. It was Rich, Terri, Bruce, and Nancy. We made our way up the bleachers to the bench behind them.

"What a surprise!" Terri turned to greet me. "Drew didn't mention he was bringing you here tonight. This is just like old times."

*Without Neil? Not quite.*

"Hi, Andrea." Nancy didn't bother to turn around. She had her eyes on Bruce or whoever else happened to be walking by. "No church meeting tonight?"

Tonight even Nancy's smart remarks didn't bother me. Although I intensely felt Neil's absence, it was good to be with my old friends again.

As we waited for the races to start, Terri snuggled close to Rich. Bruce and Nancy began to argue about some unimportant thing. It was a very familiar scene, except I was sitting beside a near stranger.

When we finally heard the announcer's voice, I settled back to watch the races and discovered Drew's arm resting along the back of the bench. It bothered me a little. I kept telling myself that it was no big deal, even when he pulled me close to his side.

Neil would have really loved the races that evening. Spin-outs and near collisions happened so often that we could never quite relax. It often gave me a good reason to break away from Drew's hold.

After the races were over, Nancy suggested we go to the Espresso, a nearby coffeehouse. I didn't want to go. I knew this crowd too well. After the Espresso, they would think of someplace else. This night could last forever.

"I should probably be getting home," I faltered. "It's getting late."

"Late? You call eleven o'clock late?" Bruce said.

"You wouldn't feel that way if Neil were here," Nancy added.

I finally allowed myself to be talked into one cup of coffee.

The coffee was still as good as I had remembered it to be, but the conversation around the table left me cold and empty.

Bruce began telling us about his most recent acid trip while Nancy lit a cigarette. Nancy kept one eye on Bruce and one eye on the door in case someone interesting walked in.

Rich and Terri acted so in love, it was embarrassing.

As for Drew, he seemed to be listening to Bruce, making an occasional comment, but he didn't take his eyes off me.

As I half listened to the conversation buzzing around me, I became very aware of my position in the group. Lately, I was on the outside looking in. I realized that it wasn't only because Neil was gone; it was because my goals, my interests, and my values had changed and these friends didn't fit into any of that.

I thought this evening could maybe be different, but here we were once again talking about things that really didn't matter.

I had enjoyed the races, but I realized that I would rather have had Grady sitting beside me. Again, I felt torn.

A terrifying scene flashed before me in vivid detail. I groped my way through a long, dark tunnel with empty blackness on every side. Behind me, I could hear the voices of Terri, Nancy, Bruce, Rich, and Drew begging me to turn around and return to the security of the past. Ahead in a barely visible circle of light stood Grady with his arms extended to me. Cheryl stood beside him. She had a wicked smile on her face and a sword in her hand. I could feel the presence of both Jesus and Neil in the tunnel, although I couldn't see, hear, or touch them. Their presence came as a gentle breeze, reassuring me I was headed in the right direction.

Drew had just mentioned at dinner tonight that the time would come when I wouldn't need "religion." He had told me that I was getting strong and that I'd be able to make it on my own soon. He thought God was only a temporary crutch.

I had no desire to argue with Drew, so I hadn't refuted his prediction. I knew he expressed the way they all felt.

They were not accepting me for who I was, but waiting for me to go back to who they expected me to be.

I finally realized that if they didn't like who I was, it was their problem, not mine. I didn't want to try to please them anymore.

"Hey, I saw this fish, you know," Bruce was saying now. "It was polka-dotted with a head like a lion's . . ."

I wondered what Grady was doing tonight. Was he thinking about me at all?

"Andrea!" Nancy spoke my name sharply.

Everyone was looking at me. Apparently they'd asked me a question that I hadn't heard.

"What?"

"We're going to the bowling alley to shoot some pool," Drew said.

"I can't," I protested. "I have to work tomorrow."

I was glad I could offer a legitimate excuse.

"See, what did I tell you?" Drew muttered. "A job is an interference, that's all. You should have listened to me."

"But I enjoy it—"

"Yuk!" Nancy blurted. "Who could enjoy working? Now I know for sure you've lost it, Andrea."

They were doing it again—putting expectations on me.

"Oh, really?" I snapped back. "Then you really ought to try 'losing it' for once. At least Jesus is there when nobody else is."

"No thanks," she returned. "It's not reality. Eventually you'll come down from your religious trip. It's going to be tough when you have to face the real world again and find out that it's just as rotten now as when you left it."

"What about your dope trips?" I countered. "You call that reality?" I turned to Drew. "Can we go please?"

He sighed and rose from the booth, pulling me after him. "I'll see you at the bowling alley later," he told them as we left.

We rode in silence most of the way home.

"I don't mind you being on your little God trip," he said as we pulled up in front of my house and cut the engine. "But why does it have to come into every conversation and ruin everything we want to do?"

I stared at Drew. He seemed to be asking an honest question, and I felt he deserved an honest answer.

"Drew, living for Jesus is not just a belief that's somehow separate from a person's everyday life. Christianity is not just something to be pulled out and displayed on Sunday mornings. Being a Christian is a lifestyle."

He still looked confused.

"There's no way you can understand what I'm saying until you've experienced it for yourself."

"If that's true, I don't want to understand. The last thing I want to be is a religious nut. And I don't think Neil would be very proud of you."

"Neil became a religious nut, as you call it, before he died. Grady was there."

"Yeah, well, at that point he didn't have anything to lose." He reached over and put his arm around my shoulders. "Hey, why don't we continue this conversation in the back where it's more comfortable?"

I removed his arm. "No. I have to go."

"Just for a few minutes?"

"No. Are you going to walk me to the door or do I have to go by myself?"

Drew hit the dashboard with his fist. "Neil never mentioned that he had to break you down first. I don't know if it's worth it." He started the engine and reached across me to open the door. "I'll wait here and make sure you get in."

"Thanks for dinner," I mumbled as I climbed out of the van.

What had Drew meant about breaking me down? What had Neil told him?

# 13

$\mathcal{I}$ missed Grady. I finally received a postcard from Canada the following week. All it said was that he was having a good time swimming in the hotel pool and doing some sight-seeing. I received another card at the end of the week. After reciting more of his itinerary, at the bottom he had scribbled in tiny handwriting that there was something he had to tell me when he returned.

What could it be? Maybe he and Cheryl had decided to date each other exclusively. How would I handle that? At least then I'd know where I stood.

Neil had never played games with my feelings like this. Maybe Grady wasn't playing a game either. More than likely he wanted to have a close friendship with me, but I was carrying it too far by assuming that he wanted more. After all, I'd referred to his cozy relationship with Cheryl many times, and he'd never once suggested that I was wrong. He'd never assured me that they weren't serious.

A sudden feeling of panic seized me at the thought of completely losing Grady's companionship. No wonder Cheryl had shot me such a nasty look. They must have talked about me the night before he'd left, trying to figure out how to deal with me. Cheryl had probably not realized the seriousness of the situation until Grady told her. What a fool I'd been. I decided to stay away from church as well as youth group. I didn't want to face any of the kids who probably knew about the situation by now, and Mr. Wagner seemed only too happy to let me work at times when Jill couldn't because of youth group activities.

The kids from youth group were usually at Tebo's and wanted to know why I was there all the time. My quick answer was that I needed the extra money. Although it was just an excuse, it was true also, and it seemed to satisfy their curiosity.

Jill let me know that she didn't buy it for a minute.

I drove up to Neil's grave often. It was the only thing that gave me comfort for the time being.

Grady would not have been happy with my obsessive thoughts of Neil. At my worst moments, I'd yell at Neil for leaving me and plead with God to let me die. No one knew, and no one seemed to care.

I stayed at home the Saturday the Hollingers returned from vacation. It took a lot for me to keep myself from trying to secretly find out what Grady and Cheryl were up to.

"Would you like to go for a drive with me and Chuck?" my mother asked that sunny July afternoon.

"No thanks," I returned without hesitation.

She shrugged. "It's too nice to stay cooped up in the house."

"You're right," I agreed. "I think I'll take a blanket and my Bible and sit out in the backyard."

"You ought to be able to find something more interesting to read around here than the Bible."

"How would you know how interesting it is? I'll bet you've never even tried reading it."

"I have tried it," she argued. "Just a bunch of names and places that don't mean anything. It's boring."

"Not if you know the One who wrote it," I smiled.

Just then Chuck knocked at the door and I opened it to let him in.

"Don't you think the Bible is an interesting book?" I asked him.

"Interesting?" He stroked his moustache. "Maybe to a Christian, but it could be very boring to the average person."

I nodded. "Exactly as I was saying."

My mother threw up her hands. "You two agree on everything." She pulled Chuck toward the door. "C'mon, before someone suggests a Bible study."

"Not a bad idea. We'll have to do that sometime," he called over his shoulder as he disappeared out the door.

I chuckled to myself as I gathered up an old blanket and the new brown leather Bible I'd bought with my first paycheck. One of these days Chuck was sure to make a decision to follow Christ again, no matter what Mom did or said.

I headed out the back door, remembering to leave a window open just in case the phone rang.

I loved the Bible. I loved to touch the soft leather. Each page felt so crisp, like a new dollar bill. At Grady's suggestion, I was reading through the Gospels. My eyes always fell on the red letters first—Jesus' words: "Do not let your hearts be troubled. Trust in God; trust also in me. In my Father's house are many rooms; if it were not so, I would have told you. I am going there to prepare a place for you. And if I go and prepare a place for you, I will come back and take you to be with me that you also may be where I am. You know the way to the place where I am going" (John 14:1–4).

How could anyone call that boring? My mother must have been reading the genealogies. Maybe if I showed her these verses it would whet her appetite.

Suddenly I heard a car pull up in our driveway. A car door slammed and then I heard footsteps. I started walking around the house and saw that it was Grady's car.

I approached the front porch and found him knocking loudly on the front door. He turned and saw me.

I don't know who made the first move, but before I realized what had happened, we were in each other's arms. He was holding me so tightly I could hardly breathe. It reminded me of my reunions with Neil after he'd been at college for a few weeks. Only Neil had smothered me with kisses.

I pulled away, confusion clouding my thoughts. What was happening? I found it hard to believe that he would hug a close friend like he'd just hugged me. I led him to my blanket in the backyard where he sat down beside me.

"Did you miss me?" he asked as he reached out for my hand.

Should I let him know how much I had missed him? I hated this stupid game. Maybe I just thought I had missed him because when I was all alone Neil's absence intensified.

"I missed you," I said.

"I missed you too."

I shifted my position, uncomfortable under his penetrating gaze.

"Tell me about your trip," I said, anxious to launch some kind of conversation.

He proceeded to tell me about the food, the people, and the places he'd toured. Then he asked me what I'd been doing in the last three weeks. This brought our small talk to an abrupt end. I told him that I'd spent most of the time sitting around doing nothing.

"I did a lot of thinking while I was gone," he began.

*Here it comes,* I thought, bracing myself for the worst.

"I wanted to talk to you about—well, we need to talk about—us."

"Us?" I repeated numbly.

He took a deep breath. "I broke up with Cheryl the night before I left. My feelings for you were so strong that—well, it wasn't fair to her. I'm not sure how you feel about me. Maybe I'm taking a risk by being so honest with you, but I just want you to know how much I care about you. You asked me if I'd ever been in love. I'm not saying that *love* is what I feel, but I know I've never felt this way about any girl before."

He hesitated and seemed to be waiting for me to respond. In my shocked state I couldn't say anything. I certainly hadn't expected anything like this.

"I know you're still hurting over Neil," he went on. "So am I, in a different way. I'm willing to wait until you can sort out your feelings. I stayed at a distance as long as I could. I kept telling myself that it was sympathy I felt for you, but I know that what I feel inside for you goes a lot deeper than sympathy."

I searched my mind frantically for a response that wouldn't sound trite or too dramatic. Maybe I should search my heart for the answer, not my mind.

"Aren't you going to say anything?" he asked.

"Grady, what you've just told me—well, I don't know what to say. I just assumed that you and Cheryl were—well, practically engaged or something. I didn't think I had a chance."

"Have you wanted a chance?" he asked. "That's what I need to know."

"Yes, I guess I have."

He reached over and softly touched his hands to my face. Then he drew back with a thoughtful look.

"I've never laid my gut feelings out in the open like this before," he said. "I've prayed about it so much that I was almost afraid God was getting bored listening to me. I really didn't believe He'd let me say so much unless you felt something too."

I wanted to assure Grady that I did, but I held back because I couldn't define what it was I felt. Did love express itself differently between different people? Neil had been exciting, but Grady was safe.

Grady didn't ask me to love him. He said he was willing

to wait. Maybe something could grow between us. As long as I didn't have to give up Neil fully, I could at least give our relationship my best shot.

"I'm not asking for any kind of commitment," Grady went on. "I don't even want to keep you from dating other guys. I just wanted you to know how I felt."

"Thank you, Grady," I faltered. "You're—you're pretty special to me too."

All of a sudden I felt as though Grady had wrapped me up in a warm, secure blanket to protect me from all the pain and hurt the world constantly offered.

"What did your mother say about your breaking up with Cheryl?" I couldn't help asking.

"She doesn't know yet. She'll find out soon enough." He squeezed my hand. "Don't worry about it. God can take care of her attitude toward you."

Grady spoke with strong conviction, but I wasn't convinced.

"Hey, before I forget . . ." He pulled a green velvet box out of his shirt pocket. "I picked up something for you in Canada."

He slowly opened the lid and hesitantly gave it to me. Inside lay a silver cross necklace.

As I turned it over in my hands, I saw our initials engraved in script on the back: Grady's on the top, mine on the bottom. "Grady, thank you. It's beautiful!"

"I wasn't sure about your taste in jewelry, but I thought it was something you might like."

"I don't really have a taste in jewelry," I admitted. "I can't afford to buy any, and this is the first time anyone has given me a necklace. Neil always gave me tapes or CDs, things like that. Once he gave me a silver-plated roach clip." I laughed. "Does that count?"

Grady wasn't laughing. His clear blue eyes remained expressionless.

Why had I said that? I felt awful.

Grady rose from the blanket. "I have some errands to do for my mother today. Do you want to come along?"

"Let me run inside and leave a note for Mom."

Grady waited for me in the car. As we drove away, I decided to keep thoughts of my relationship with Neil to myself.

*Neil, you know how I feel about you, how I'll always feel about you.* No one else has to know. I pictured Neil somewhere in heaven, smiling as he looked down on me and his little brother. More than anything, I wanted him to approve.

# 14

The month of August arrived. For days the temperature never dropped below 90 degrees until the sun went down.

Grady took me to the river practically every day after work. Marc and Jill came with us sometimes, but mostly we went by ourselves.

Grady and I really got to know each other. We swam and played in the water, and then we would sit on the sandy beach and talk for hours.

"I love sauerkraut." Grady licked his lips as we talked about our favorite foods.

"Did your mother fix sauerkraut when Neil was alive?" I asked. "Neil hated sauerkraut."

He nodded. "I know. She made it sometimes with polish sausage."

Another time he told me about the 283 engine he was putting into his Chevy.

"That's the best one," I said. "It's the one Neil would have chosen."

"I learned most everything I know about cars from Neil."

"You're a lot like him in many ways," I couldn't help adding, knowing he would be complimented.

"Yeah, but in a lot of ways I'm different!" he snapped back. "I love sauerkraut, remember?"

With that, he dove into the water, leaving me alone on

the beach. *What brought that on?* I wondered.

Grady apologized later. He blamed his remark on the hot day. I wasn't sure I believed him.

Jill and I decided to quit work a couple of weeks before school started to give us some time to goof off. On our last workday we treated ourselves to a pizza at an Italian restaurant down the block.

"I really appreciate your getting me this job," I told her when we were seated at a table. "It helped pass the time this summer."

"It's been fun working together," Jill returned. "I can hardly believe it's time for school to start."

"Yeah," I sighed. "But I'll always remember this summer. On one hand, it's been my worst summer ever because of losing Neil. On the other hand, it's the best because of finding Jesus." I paused before I continued. "Then there's Grady—God was so good to give me someone to take Neil's place. I mean, Grady is the next best thing to Neil. I'd have gone crazy without him."

That didn't sound any better. How would I get out of this?

"Grady wouldn't consider that a compliment," Jill affirmed.

"I didn't say it to Grady," I returned impatiently. "I don't have to. He understands that Neil will always be number one."

"He might understand it," she acknowledged. "But that doesn't mean he likes it. How would you like to be number two in his life? Second to Cheryl Riley, for instance?"

"That's different. She's alive."

"It's the same thing," Jill argued. "It's still second place. Grady won't put up with this for long." She sighed. "You and Grady could have such an incredible relationship if you would just let go of Neil."

I shook my head. "I don't see it that way at all. My love

for Neil isn't affecting Grady. You're imagining things. Let's change the subject." I changed position, searching uneasily for something to say. "Are you going to the church picnic next weekend?"

She nodded.

"It sounds like fun. I think I'll ask my friend Terri to come with me."

I tried to forget about our conversation as we returned to work.

Let go of Neil—who was she kidding? That was easy for her to say. She had Marc's love. Let him be snatched away from her, and I wondered if she'd be able to take her own advice.

One morning, a few days later, I dropped by Terri's house. She was still in her robe when she answered the door. "Andrea!" she cried. "You're the last person I expected to see this morning."

I followed her to her bedroom. She proceeded to get dressed.

"You're probably wondering why I'm still in my robe when it's almost noon."

I hadn't been wondering at all, but she seemed anxious to tell me.

"I've been sick just about every morning for the last two weeks," she went on. "It's all I can do to drag myself out of bed." She looked around the room, avoiding eye contact. "I don't think Rich and I were careful enough. I think I might be pregnant."

"Oh, Terri!" I eyed her sympathetically.

Terri had always feared pregnancy. She didn't want to lose Rich, and she was scared that if she ever got pregnant, he'd say goodbye.

"Have you told Rich?" I asked.

"No—and don't you dare say a word to anyone. You're the only person I've told. I have a doctor's appointment this

Thursday. Maybe it's just the flu." She smiled weakly. "I hope."

"I'm sure sorry—"

"Don't be sorry until after Thursday. If I'm pregnant, we can worry together." She lit a cigarette.

"Rich will be here soon. He'll be glad to see you. We've missed seeing you around. I suppose you're busy with Grady and your job."

"Yeah. I'm involved in a lot of activities at my church too. We're having a picnic next Saturday. I was wondering if you'd go with me. I'd like you to meet some of my guy friends."

"Next Saturday?" Terri checked over a date calendar on her desk. "What are you going to do there?"

"Oh, eat, play games, eat, have relays, eat some more."

"Sounds good." She frowned. "I've been awfully hungry lately."

The doorbell rang and I followed Terri to the door.

When the door opened, I wanted to hide. Right behind Rich stood Drew. I hadn't seen him since our last date. I had hoped to avoid him as long as I could.

"Hi," Rich greeted us. "Drew wanted to say goodbye. He's leaving tonight for school."

"Hi, Andrea," Drew grinned. "What a nice surprise. I didn't know you'd be here."

"You wouldn't have come if you'd known?"

"Oh, I'm not so sure about that—"

"Hey, what's going on?" Rich asked.

"Nothing that a burger and a shake won't cure." Drew grabbed my hand. "Let's go to Smitty's. I'm starved."

How could I get out of this? I belonged to Grady now, didn't I? He hadn't actually said so, but it had been implied. Eating lunch with Drew was no big deal, but someone might see us and get the wrong impression. Maybe I could suggest a different restaurant where we wouldn't run into anyone we knew.

What kind of a way was this for Grady and me to start off our new relationship? It wouldn't be right for me to sneak off to a restaurant with Drew Bradshaw. I didn't even want to eat lunch with him. It was about time I started thinking for myself.

We were climbing into Rich's car when I pulled my hand free from Drew's and backed off.

"I'm sorry, but I can't go," I said. "I just remembered I promised my mother I'd start dinner at one o'clock."

Drew frowned. "We'll be back by then."

"I have to stop at the store first. I'm sorry. It was good to see you, Drew. Have a great year at college. I'll see you on Saturday, Terri."

"Hey, wait a minute—" Drew began.

I climbed into my car and heard Drew swear as I drove off. My refusal to go to lunch had been less than diplomatic, but I knew I'd done the right thing. Drew would get over it. I hadn't told a lie either. Grady and Chuck were coming for dinner and I'd promised to make stew. I hoped Grady would be as crazy about my stew as Neil had been.

I'd never before attempted to make the stew by myself, but Mom had gone somewhere with Chuck and wouldn't be back until five. The meat was supposed to simmer for a while.

Grady pulled into the driveway before I'd even unpacked the grocery bags. I'd certainly made the right decision in not going with Drew.

I waved to Grady through the kitchen window and let him in the back door.

"I know I'm four hours early." He grinned. "But I couldn't wait that long to see you." He came up behind me and put his hands on my shoulders.

"Oh? Any special reason?"

"No." He turned me around and kissed me. "Can I help?"

I handed him a knife. "You can cut up the roast while I put the vegetables away."

"Does Chuck have any plans after dinner?" Grady asked.

"I don't know. Why?"

"There's an antique auto show at the coliseum. I don't know about your mom, but Chuck would enjoy it."

"That sounds like fun. Let's ask them."

As the meat simmered, we watched an old Spencer Tracy movie on television. When it ended, we returned to the kitchen to start cutting the vegetables.

"You're kidding!" Grady exclaimed as he watched me pile all the vegetables on the counter. "You put all that in stew?"

"Sure. I just hope I'm not forgetting anything."

"I'll bet it's delicious."

"It is," I assured him and held up two rutabagas. "I wonder if I should put these in. Neil never liked them. He always picked them out."

"Does that mean I have to pick mine out?" Grady asked.

"Of course not. I just don't want you feeling like you have to eat something you don't like."

"I like rutabagas."

"Good. Here's a fat one." I threw it to him. "Peel it, cut it up, and drop it in."

We were butchering the onions, laughing and crying at the same time, when Chuck and my mom showed up.

"What in the world are you doing?" Mom asked before she saw the onions. "Oh, I see. For a minute, I thought you'd both gone crazy."

The stew's delicious aroma filled every corner of the house. I watched Grady and Chuck play a game of Chess while my mother leafed through the newspaper. I couldn't remember when our house had seemed so much like a home, even when Neil was alive.

Neil had never stuck around long enough to get to know Chuck. He hadn't bothered with my mother's boyfriends. Not that I blamed him. Most of them proved to be real bores. Assuming Chuck to be the same, we'd never really given him a chance. But Grady treated Chuck special, just as he treated everyone.

We all raved over the stew. It truly did seem to taste better tonight than ever before. Maybe because we'd made it all by ourselves.

When Grady mentioned the Auto Show, my mother and Chuck both looked interested.

"Oh, I love old cars!" Mom exclaimed. "Andrea's grandpa used to have dozens of them on the farm we lived on back in Nebraska. He was always going to fix them up and sell them, but he never did. They just kept accumulating. We played in them a lot."

That was news to me. I could hardly picture my mother as a little girl.

After cleaning up the dishes together, we climbed into Chuck's station wagon. A double date with my mother and her boyfriend. *Neil, you would never believe this. . . .*

# 15

*I* never would have imagined that looking at old cars could be so much fun. I'm not sure I would have had so much fun had Chuck and Mom not gone along.

Since Grady had come into my life, I was spending more time with my mother than ever before. We were learning how to enjoy each other's company.

Neil had always told me to disregard the older generation and their views. I had followed his philosophy, mainly because most of the adults I knew seemed to disapprove of our lifestyle. Neil had come under constant attack from his parents, and although Mom was silent much of the time, I knew she too didn't like my behavior or my friends.

Maybe I had never let her get to know me. It was obvious that this was the case when I mentioned a class in anthropology I'd be taking in my fall schedule at school. She was completely surprised.

"I never knew you were interested in anthropology."

"Isn't everyone?" I answered.

"I suppose, but I just never—I didn't realize you ever thought about such things."

She looked at me as if by some great revelation she suddenly realized I was a thinking, feeling human being instead of simply a rebellious teenager.

"We need to talk more," she said thoughtfully as she picked a piece of lint off my sweater.

For once I agreed.

The opportunity presented itself that very evening after Chuck and Grady had gone home. Mom flopped into the overstuffed chair in the living room and announced that Chuck had asked her to marry him.

"Oh?" My heart stopped for a second, and I almost dropped the coat hanger I was using to hang up my jacket. I closed the closet door and leaned against it.

"And what did you say?"

*Why was I so surprised? Most of her boyfriends had eventually suggested marriage.* Usually she was not interested in "that particular ritualistic act" as she expressed it. This time I wasn't so sure.

"Nothing," she returned. "The idea is so new to me. I'll have to think about it. I know what I'd like to say."

That's what I was afraid of.

"You love him, don't you?"

"Yes, I think so. You and I have been alone for nine years. I wonder if we could adjust to having a man around again. At least now I can tell Chuck to go home if I don't want him around."

I smiled. I liked Chuck, but I didn't know what I thought about having him around as a permanent fixture.

"How do you feel about it?" Mom asked.

There was a time when my mother couldn't have cared less how I felt about anything. Things were truly changing between us. I wasn't sure how I felt, but I swallowed the words that tried to fight their way out of my mouth. This had to be her decision.

"My opinion isn't what's important, Mom," I said slowly. "If you love him—I . . . I think he'd be a good husband, don't you?"

She quickly jumped out of her chair and hugged me. I couldn't remember the last time she had held me. "Oh, Andrea, I believe he would. I really do. I believe he'd be good to you too."

She twirled around and kind of floated into her bedroom, saying, "You can help me pick out a dress pattern this week."

Chuck as my stepfather. Surely I'd get used to the idea. It wouldn't be that different. Most of the time, whenever my mother was home, he was here too. I knew he wasn't the type of person who would take advantage of his new role as an authority figure in my life and use it to try to control me. He'd always been one to let me know his feelings about anything that concerned me, even more so than Mom did. Yet he managed to do it without forcing me to see things his way.

He must really love my mother to want to marry her. I couldn't help but wonder what he had done with the love he felt for his first wife.

I asked him about it a few nights later when Mom had gone to the store and we were alone at the dining room table munching on potato chips.

"I still love Carolyn," Chuck told me. "But in a different way than I love your mother. They aren't in competition."

I shook my head. "I don't understand that at all. You can't love two people at the same time."

"Do you love your mother?" Chuck asked.

"Of course."

"Do you love Neil?"

"Yes, of course, but that's different."

"That's exactly what I said." Chuck leaned toward me. "It's different."

"What if Mom gets tired of you and falls for someone else?" I blurted out. "Worse yet, what if she dies? You'll be sorry then, right?"

"Wrong," Chuck said softly. "I'll be grateful for the time we had together. That's the risk you take when you love, Andrea."

Now it was my turn to lean forward. "No way. I'm not

going through that again, ever."

Chuck shrugged. "That's your choice, but I'm afraid you'll be the loser."

"I won't feel any pain if I don't let myself fall for anyone else the way I did for Neil."

"Don't be so sure." Chuck's eyes narrowed. "I've been there."

"It's all Neil's fault." I felt the familiar swelling sensation in my throat making it difficult to speak. "The hurt just never goes away, Chuck."

"Yes, it does." Chuck took both my hands and squeezed them in his own. "That too is your choice."

Chuck was the one person to whom I couldn't say, "You don't understand."

———

When I awoke on Saturday morning, I ran immediately to the window to see what the weather was like. It had been cooler the last few days, a sign that summer was ending and autumn was quickly approaching.

The sun shone through the clouds, and I knew it was only a matter of time until it would be hot enough to go swimming at the church picnic. I had promised Grady that I'd meet him at the park, but I first wanted to have some time alone with Terri. It had been so long since we'd had the chance to talk without a lot of distractions and interruptions—Rich being the main one.

I was anxious for her to see me in my new setting with my new friends, and I hoped that it would appeal to her. Maybe she would see that life offered more than partying, booze, drugs, and sex. Without the input of the old group, maybe I could help her think for herself.

I jumped into a pair of jeans and pulled a T-shirt over my head. Slipping a pair of sandals on my feet, I yelled goodbye to my mother and ran out the door.

When I parked in Terri's driveway and honked the horn, she didn't appear right away as she usually did. I honked again.

When she finally stuck her head out the door, she looked puzzled.

"You're coming to the picnic with me, aren't you?" I asked.

She frowned. "Picnic? Oh, yeah, you did invite me to a picnic today. Slipped my mind. I'm not sure I can go, Andrea."

Terri acted as if she had a lot on her mind. She'd never before forgotten any plans we had together.

"Why not?"

"Rich is coming over and I think we're going to do something," she returned. "He didn't mention anything specific."

"Can't you call him and tell him you're going to the picnic? We haven't done anything together for so long."

"Yeah, I suppose I could call him."

She disappeared into the house and I waited—and waited. Finally she reappeared, scowling slightly, and climbed into the car.

"He wasn't happy," she told me. "I promised him I'd stay only a couple of hours. He's picking me up at noon."

"Oh, great," I muttered. "That's about when it gets exciting."

"Exciting?" Terri laughed. "How exciting can a church picnic get?"

"You're beginning to sound like Nancy."

"I'm sorry," she apologized. "I just haven't been in a good mood lately. Guess why."

"You're pregnant for sure, then?"

She nodded.

"Are you going to get married?"

Terri shrugged. "Who can plan that far ahead? Maybe

someday. We'll probably live together first. Right now it looks like the only thing to do is to get an abortion."

I kept myself from gasping out loud. Was this Terri talking? It couldn't be. I remembered the many times we'd talked about getting married and having babies. When Rich and Neil came into the picture, we planned on moving next door to each other and living happily ever after with our handsome husbands and beautiful children.

"You can't do that," I said quietly.

"I wish there were some other way, but we've gone over every possibility. This is the most convenient."

How could it be more "convenient" to kill another human being?

I shook my head. "I know you too well, Terri. I can't believe you would kill a child that you and Rich together—"

"It's not a baby—not yet."

"That's not true. The Bible says God knew us when we where in our mother's womb. If we were nothings, He couldn't have known us."

Fortunately we had recently discussed abortion at a youth meeting, and I had learned quite a bit about God's view on the subject.

Terri was silent for a moment.

"Just between you and me," she said thoughtfully, "I don't know if I can go through with it. I'm hoping Rich will change his mind. He's still the most important person to me—more important than this—whatever you call it inside of me."

We parked in front of the park grounds and climbed out. Grady came running the minute he saw us. I was so proud of him. Wearing a pair of cutoffs and a T-shirt, he looked tanned and muscular.

"Hi, Terri," Grady greeted warmly as he put my arm through his. "I'm glad you could come. Let's go get some Cokes."

Terri hung back as we joined the large group of kids gathered around the picnic table, which was piled high with soft drinks. I introduced Terri to as many people as I knew, Cheryl included. Grady's former girlfriend stayed a safe distance away from me, but she didn't act hostile toward me now. I supposed we'd never be the best of friends, but at least I wasn't afraid of her anymore.

Terri seemed uncomfortable. Maybe she was just pre-occupied with being pregnant. Then some of the kids formed teams for volleyball and asked us to join them.

"Would you like to play?" I asked her.

"I'd better not," she refused. "I might jar something loose."

"Let's go find a shady spot and sit down then," I suggested, feeling the sun's rays beating down on my shoulders.

"You don't mind if I go play some football, do you?" Grady asked.

"Go ahead. We'll be sitting over here." I pointed to a bush a few feet away.

"You seem to have gotten a hook into him," Terri observed as we sat down.

I smiled. "He's sweet."

Terri shook her head and shuddered slightly. "I don't see how you do it."

"Do what?"

"Date Neil's little brother. It's weird. Besides, it seems like you'd always be comparing them."

I shrugged. "I guess I do. I don't see how that can be helped."

"Well, I know how you felt about Neil. Doesn't Grady tend to come out on the short end?"

"Oh, I don't know. I've realized that they're really quite different from each other."

"That's obvious. That's what I don't get. How can you date someone so completely opposite from Neil?"

"Because I lost Neil and I need Grady." Why did I always have to defend my relationship with Grady? "We need each other right now."

"What? You could form a Neil Hollinger fan club and accomplish the same thing. I'd even join. I miss him too. You certainly can't use another person like you would use a Band-Aid."

I got up quickly. I could do without Terri's advice.

"Let's go watch the guys play football." I began walking.

"Hey, I didn't mean anything," Terri said as she caught up with me. "I just meant—well—"

"Forget it. It's not the first time I've heard that."

Terri's company was boring that morning. She seemed distant and hard to talk to. We couldn't get involved in the games because she didn't want to do anything strenuous. I was beginning to wonder if she had any life in her at all when Rich showed up.

"Ready?" he asked Terri as he eyed the food spread over three picnic tables.

Terri clung to him as if she thought he might run away any minute. She nodded.

Grady broke away from his football game to join us.

"Hi, Rich. You're staying to eat with us, aren't you?"

Rich took another look at the food and licked his lips hungrily. "It does look good." He glanced at Terri. "You want to stay?"

"Why not," Terri conceded.

The conversation at lunch centered mostly around school and football. Both Grady and Rich held first-string positions on the school team. Apparently they knew each other pretty well. Grady persuaded Rich to stay and play ball after lunch. Terri seemed more relaxed once Rich arrived, and she didn't seem to mind staying.

We walked by the creek while the guys played football.

"Is it getting any easier?" Terri asked. "I mean—life without Neil."

"It's hard to tell. The days all kind of merge together." I swallowed hard and continued. "But being able to pray and knowing that God cares has helped a lot. Seriously, Terri, you wouldn't have to be so afraid of losing Rich or having a baby or anything for that matter if you knew Jesus. When God is in control of your life, things seem to work out somehow."

"I've been thinking about that," Terri admitted.

"Have you come to any conclusions?" I asked.

She kicked a stone along the path in front of her. "Not really. Rich and I have talked about it. I guess when you're going to have a baby and marriage becomes a possibility, you begin to grow up."

She was thinking about God, and that was important.

I began to realize that it wasn't Terri I needed to worry about. It was Rich. He had a lot of power over her. If he could convince her that it was convenient to have an abortion, he could also prevent her from making a decision for God. Yes, it was Rich I needed to worry about.

# 16

School started the following week. Everyone knew about Neil's death, but not many knew about my relationship with Grady. Some didn't bother to hide their surprise when they saw us together. They remembered me the way I was before I had met Christ, and they couldn't understand the basis for my relationship with Grady.

When I began to tell some of them about Jesus, I got a few shrugs, a few raised eyebrows, and some outright laughs. It didn't surprise me. I'd thought Christianity was weird too before I understood what it was all about. Now that I knew Jesus, I couldn't see how I ever lived without Him.

I was proud to be Grady's girl, even though the guys in my class didn't approve. Those who had known Neil offered their opinion on the matter.

"Grady's not your type at all," one guy told me. "You're just using him, aren't you?"

"He's nothing like Neil, so why waste your time?" another added.

I tried to ignore them, but it began to trouble me. I wondered if Grady was getting similar treatment.

As I waited for Grady to put his books in his locker one day after football practice, I decided to ask him about it. It was late afternoon and the halls were deserted.

"Some of the guys think I'm just using you, Grady," I said casually.

He pulled out a trigonometry book from his stack of textbooks and closed the locker door. He then stood and looked at me for a moment. What was he thinking? Maybe I shouldn't have said anything.

"Are you?" he asked finally.

"What? Of course not. How could you even ask that?"

He shrugged. "I guess I find it hard to believe that you could care about me as much as I care about you. Besides, I can't compete with Neil."

"You're not competing with Neil," I reassured him. "I care about you in a different way."

"Yeah, that's obvious," he said grimly. "I remember how you and Neil couldn't keep your hands off each other. The way you act when I try to touch you—you'd think I had a disease or something."

"I've never said anything to make you think—"

"You don't have to say anything," he interrupted. "I can feel it."

He was right. For some reason, I couldn't shake the uneasiness I felt whenever Grady touched me. How did I know that Neil wasn't somehow watching? Not only that, but I didn't want anyone else to touch me in the way Neil had. I couldn't love another person the way I loved Neil.

"I'm sorry, Grady," I mumbled, not knowing what else to say.

"I'm glad you brought this up," Grady went on. "It's been bothering me for a long time. If you're sorry, do something about it. I don't really want your apologies—I want it to change." His eyes pleaded with me. "Can't we just put the past behind us?"

I shook my head violently. "You don't know what you're asking. How can you expect me to—it's only been four months."

Grady threw up his hands. "You'll be saying that a year

from now. How long are you going to hang on to someone who's not here?"

I glared at him and struggled not to cry. "You're mean, Grady Hollinger. I thought you understood, but you don't. You don't understand at all."

Grady touched my shoulder, but when I remained stiff, he let his arm drop to his side.

"I'm trying to understand. Don't you think I loved him too?"

"I know you did." I sniffed. "I guess a brother's love is different than a girlfriend's."

"It must be."

After that day, Neil was seldom mentioned in our conversations.

I saw less and less of Grady as the football season peaked. Practices and Friday night games kept him busy. We dated on Saturday nights and we occasionally saw each other at school and church activities. Our relationship seemed lighter after that conversation about Neil. It was almost a relief. I felt as if the pressure had been lifted. Now in order to protect what we did have, we seemed to be hiding our true feelings and thoughts from each other.

I had always looked forward to my senior year—the games, parties, and school functions. Though I stayed in the center of activity most of the time, I still felt very alone.

If only I had someone to talk to. My mother was all caught up with wedding plans. She and Chuck had set a date for some time in January. Recently, she had enough time to say hello, but never long enough to hear my cries for help. It was just as well. I had truly come to love my mom and didn't want to be the one to wreck the joy she felt in her decision to marry Chuck.

I hadn't heard anything from Drew since he'd gone back to school. That was fine with me. He reminded me too much of Neil and my old lifestyle.

It was on a Friday night after a football game that Grady and I ran into him at Smitty's. We usually didn't go there, but it was late and we stopped by on the way home. I immediately noticed him sitting in the back with a couple of guys. I kept my back turned to him, hoping he wouldn't see me. Before I knew it, I felt a hand on my arm.

"Hi there, sweetheart," he said, ignoring Grady.

"Hi, Drew." I looked into his eyes, which appeared dull and glazed over.

"It's good to see you," he went on. "It's been too long."

He clutched my arm tighter and I tried to free myself.

"C'mon, Andrea," Grady pulled me toward himself.

"Hang on, Hollinger," Drew growled. "Whatever you two have planned can wait. If what Neil told me about this little lady is true, you have quite an evening ahead of you." He chuckled softly.

I jerked my arm free and glared at him. I wasn't sure what he meant, but I wasn't about to ask. Grady and I turned and walked out.

"The guy's a no-good bum," Grady muttered as we drove away.

"Oh, Drew's not a bad guy when he's straight." I tried to defend him. I felt as if Grady was implying that Neil used bad judgment in choosing friends.

"Then maybe I've never seen him when he's straight."

"He was Neil's best friend," I persisted. "He can't be all bad."

"That doesn't mean anything," Grady argued. "Neil had some real weirdos for friends."

"Well, I guess we all have some weirdos for friends, don't we? I don't think much of your friend Cheryl Riley."

Grady grinned. "Do I detect a hint of jealousy?"

I shrugged. "What do I have to be jealous about? She's got it in for me, that's all. She's turned the whole youth group against me."

Grady frowned. "Andrea, that's not true. They love you."

"They haven't gone out of their way to be friendly," I complained.

"I don't see you going much out of your way either. Some of them have tried to talk to you, tried to make friends, but you stay in your little world of self-pity. You won't let anyone else in. There's only room for you and my brother."

"I've let God in," I said defensively.

"Have you?" Grady stopped the car in the driveway of my house. "Have you really?"

I bit my lip to keep from crying. Grady must be sick of seeing me cry. He leaned against the door and looked at me for a moment. "I'm sorry, Andrea. I just want to be in your life so badly I can hardly stand it. If you only knew how much you mean to me."

"Grady, I don't mean to hurt you and I don't want to lose you. I do need you."

"You need me," Grady repeated dully as he stared out the window.

"It's more than just a need," I added quickly.

"Is it?"

Not wanting to explain myself further, I opened my door to get out. Grady jumped out and hurried around the car to meet me. We approached the front porch and I turned to him. "You really are important to me." I tried once more to reassure him.

"I know. It's okay. Forget it."

I knew it wasn't okay when I noticed the slump of his shoulders as he walked back down the drive.

The next day Mom asked me to go on some errands with her. I was ready to do anything to take my mind off my problems.

As I waited for her in the car, an unexpected visitor

came. Drew roared to a stop right beside the car. He smiled crookedly, and I reluctantly rolled down the window.

"We're going to the bike races today. Want to come along? It'll be a blast, like old times—almost. Neil won't be there, of course . . ." He hesitated.

Drew missed him too.

"Nancy and Bruce are going," he went on. "And Rich and Terri, but they're not going to ride. She's like this, you know." He formed a circle with his hands in front of his stomach. "You want to go?"

"I can't, Drew. I promised my mom I'd do some errands with her."

"Can't they wait?" He looked disappointed.

I shook my head. "I'm sorry."

He shrugged. "That's too bad." He punched the throttle. "See you later."

I couldn't give Drew any encouragement at all. I wouldn't do anything more to jeopardize my relationship with Grady. Now that football season was almost over, we were beginning to see more of each other.

I still felt the Hollingers' disapproval of our relationship. I was polite to Mrs. Hollinger when we happened to meet at church, but I tried to avoid her whenever possible.

One Sunday morning in mid-November she stopped me outside the church.

"Andrea, if you and your mother aren't busy on Thanksgiving, we'd like you to join us for dinner."

"Oh—well—th-thank you," I stammered. "I think my mother is going to be with Chuck and his family. I was going to tag along, but I'm sure she won't mind if I come to your house instead."

Grady, who stood a little behind her, beamed with approval.

"Wonderful. We'll eat around four o'clock."

She turned to talk to some other people, and I drew Grady aside.

"Grady, why? What's her motive? I can't go through another evening like the last one."

"It won't be like that," Grady promised. "I think she wants to get to know you. Maybe she's realized she can't fight against us anymore."

I wasn't so sure. I didn't trust Mrs. Hollinger, but for the sake of everyone involved, I'd go through with it.

It couldn't be worse than the previous Thanksgiving when I had spent the day at the Hollingers with Neil and some of his relatives. She didn't speak one word to me the whole day.

But maybe this year would be different.

# 17

$\mathscr{I}$ wandered around our house trying desperately to find something to occupy my time. It was the Saturday before Thanksgiving, and loneliness seemed to surround me.

Mom had gone shopping with a friend. Grady and Marc were checking around junkyards looking for a door panel for Marc's car. I'd called both Terri and Jill, but they were busy.

As I thought about celebrating Thanksgiving and then Christmas without Neil, I suddenly missed him so much I couldn't stand it. I decided to drive out to the cemetery.

I always enjoyed this drive. I loved to breathe the country air, and I enjoyed driving by the little farmhouses set apart by apple orchards or herds of grazing cows.

When I arrived at the cemetery, it looked deserted. During the summer I'd always found a few people milling around. I parked my car, relishing the first few moments of silence. I gladly welcomed the quiet after the constant noise and loud traffic of the city.

I knelt on the cold, hard granite of Neil's tombstone and gazed out at the rolling hills below.

A small boy ran through a field grasping the string of a kite which was soaring high above him. I wanted to be a child again—free from heartache. Why was growing up so difficult?

"Neil, I still love you so much," my voice trembled. "You're in my thoughts constantly. If I knew of an easy way to lie down here and die so I could be with you, I'd do it."

I stopped talking and let my imagination take over. Neil's handsome features remained crystal clear in my memory. I remembered the natural wave of his brown hair as it curled around the back of his neck. I would never forget the crinkles at the corners of his laughing eyes.

In contrast to Grady's soft, tender way of speaking, Neil's voice was loud and full of authority. People listened to him.

"Neil, it's not fair!" I screamed.

I could scream forever, but he'd never answer me. Neil was dead, completely and finally dead.

My mind knew the truth and continually struggled with my resisting heart. I didn't know how to live without Neil. If Neil couldn't hear me, maybe God could.

"God, it's not fair," I said aloud.

"Let go." I turned around to see who had spoken. I saw no one.

"God, is that you?" I asked softly.

"Let go of Neil."

There it was again, more specific. It seemed like a voice speaking inside of my head somewhere. Was I going crazy? I wouldn't be surprised after these last few months of torment. I knew in my heart that God was trying to get through to me. I just didn't like what He was saying. I didn't want to hear it.

"It's time to quit crying and begin to live once again."

"But I can't live without Neil!" I cried aloud.

I lifted my head and noticed an old oak tree nearby, bare except for a few leaves that had stubbornly refused to let go. The analogy became clear in my mind that unless the leaves cooperated, the tree couldn't produce new leaves this spring.

I remembered a scripture verse we'd discussed at youth group. "Unless a kernel of wheat falls to the ground and dies, it remains only a single seed. But if it dies, it produces many seeds" (John 12:24).

I tried to gather my cluttered thoughts into some kind of reasonable order. I wouldn't let Neil go. Why everyone insisted that I needed to let him go remained a mystery to me. When someone dies, do you just go on as though they never existed? How ridiculous.

Yet maybe it's the only method of survival. Certainly I would eventually drive myself crazy with thoughts and desires for Neil. I would never be satisfied.

I stood to my feet. My brain was reeling with confusion, but I was glad that I could no longer hear the voice that contradicted my feelings. I trudged back to the car.

Inside of my car, I turned on the radio in an attempt to free my mind from the agony of memories. A favorite song of mine and Neil's blared out. *I couldn't get away from Neil even if I tried,* I thought happily.

I stopped for a hamburger at Smitty's on the way home. As I waited for my order, I heard someone in the back call my name. I turned to see Nancy waving at me. When they brought my hamburger, I walked over and squeezed into the booth beside her and Bruce. Another couple sat across from us and more of the gang hovered nearby. Everyone seemed glad to see me.

"So how's the little religious girl?" Bruce asked with a teasing wink. "We've missed your funny face."

"Oh, I've been busy."

"Yeah, I'll bet," Bruce snickered. "We've heard about your hot romance with Neil's little brother."

"It couldn't be too hot," someone chuckled. "He's a religious nut like his folks."

*Defend Grady, you dummy,* something inside of me prodded. I kept my mouth shut.

"So what's he got?" Bruce asked.

"None of your business."

"That bad, huh?" Nancy clucked her tongue. "Why don't you give Drew a try? He really likes you."

"Drew's all right." I shrugged noncommittally. "But he's not Neil."

Everyone became instantly quiet. I hadn't meant to put a damper on anyone. I was only expressing my feelings.

"Guess you're out of luck there, sweetheart," Bruce mumbled finally. "Neil doesn't have much to offer you anymore, except heartache and broken dreams—that's not his fault, of course. Do yourself a favor and forget about him. Life goes on, you know?"

Does it? Even Neil's closest friends didn't understand. Why was it so hard for me to let go? They didn't seem to have any trouble.

When I saw Drew stride in the door, I decided it was time to leave.

He towered over our table before I had a chance to get away. As I rose to my feet, he gently sat me back down.

"Not so fast, beautiful." Everyone squeezed together even more to make room for Drew. "How do we rate to have the lovely presence of Andrea Lyons in our midst?" he asked no one in particular.

"It wasn't easy," Nancy drawled. "We bribed her, told her you might take her out soon."

"All right," Drew said. "How about tonight?"

"I have plans. Sorry."

"So do I. Is little Hollinger still keeping you busy?"

I nodded.

Drew shook his head. "What's he got that I don't?"

"Hollinger blood," Nancy quipped.

I'd had enough. I nudged Drew. "Excuse me, please."

No one said goodbye. When I got outside, I realized that Drew had followed me.

"I'm sorry again," Drew apologized. "Nancy has no tact."

I almost told him that at times his lack of tact was just as bad, but I stopped myself in time.

"You're not mad, are you?" he asked.

I shook my head.

"I'm not home many weekends. Couldn't you put Hollinger off one Saturday night?"

It was time to level with him. "Drew, you and I are going in two different directions. I'm not the same person I used to be. If you knew me better, you'd understand that. I'm not your type."

"Oh, yeah?" Drew grinned. "You're sure about that? What is my type?"

"Never mind. I've got to be going."

He sighed. "I guess Grady's got you all tied up."

I didn't bother to correct him that it was Neil, not Grady, who had me tied up.

"See you, Drew," I called as I climbed into the car.

"Bye." Drew shoved his hands into his pockets and disappeared into Smitty's.

The phone was ringing when I got in the door at home.

"Where have you been?" Grady asked when I answered. "I've been calling all day."

I was taken by surprise. "I . . . I went up to the cemetery."

"Oh." He was silent. "How's Neil?"

"Oh, Grady, what kind of a question is that?"

"A dumb one," he admitted. "Look, I promised my parents I'd ride out with them to visit my grandfather. We're spending the night, so I won't be able to come over tonight. I'll make it up to you next weekend."

"Okay."

Mom didn't have a date with Chuck, so we spent a nice quiet evening at home talking. We'd grown closer, and conversation came a lot easier now. I credited Chuck with at least part of our new closeness. He'd helped my mother understand that Christianity wasn't for weirdos. Realizing the change she'd seen in me, she'd been forced to agree.

I had to hand it to Chuck. He knew how to build a solid case. I continued to hope and pray that Chuck would join the ranks himself and that my mother would eventually accept it as the best for her also.

Thanksgiving Day came quickly. I suppose it arrived so fast because I'd pushed it out of mind, hoping that if I didn't think about it, maybe it wouldn't come. I didn't relish the idea of spending the day with Mrs. Hollinger, but I looked forward to seeing Grady.

As I pulled into the Hollingers' long circular driveway, there were a number of cars parked there already. Obviously it wasn't going to be just the four of us. I was grateful.

Grady met me at the door. "I'm glad you're here. I was afraid maybe you decided not to come after all."

"The thought did cross my mind," I admitted.

Grady smiled and began to take me through the room, introducing me to some of his relatives as we made our way to the kitchen to greet Mrs. Hollinger. I remembered being introduced to a few of them when I was Neil's girlfriend. They eyed me curiously now like they were trying to remember where they'd met me before.

Mrs. Hollinger turned from the stove when we walked in. "Hello, Andrea. I'm pleased you could join us. Have you introduced Andrea around, Grady?"

"A little," he answered.

"Make sure she meets everyone. We'll be eating in a few minutes."

Mrs. Hollinger, a gourmet cook, had prepared an elaborate table, spread with various vegetable dishes and salads which surrounded the huge turkey in the center. After Mr. Hollinger asked the blessing, we circled the table and then sat down wherever we wanted.

I suspected Mrs. Hollinger was up to something. She

asked me twice if I had enough to eat and refilled my juice glass three times. Maybe she just wanted to look good in front of her relatives. When I went to the kitchen to rinse my plate, she followed me.

"Are you enjoying yourself?" she asked.

"Why, yes, I am, thank you."

"Andrea, I finally made myself clean Neil's room out the other day. It was an extremely difficult thing for me to have to do. I came across picture after picture of you, letters, cards . . . he must have cared for you very much to keep them tucked away like he did."

"We had a very special relationship."

"I have much to be thankful for this Thanksgiving." She nervously began to rinse out some of the pots in the sink. "I have a wonderful husband, my friends, my church, a beautiful home—I have Grady. I'm realizing the incredible pressure I've placed upon him to be everything I've ever wanted in a son . . . because he's my only son." Her voice cracked. I began to help her with the dishes, but after sending two lids clattering into the sink, I stepped back, continuing to wonder why in the world she was telling me all of this.

"You see, to me, you and Neil always symbolized rebellious youth. It absolutely terrified me when Grady began to date you. I assumed your conversion was simply a front for Grady's sake."

"Oh, but that's not true!" I defended.

"I know that now," she said kindly. "That's what I'm trying to say. I believe I've judged you unfairly and I want you to know I'm terribly sorry. I won't be interfering in your relationship with my son anymore."

I couldn't think of anything to say. Why did my mind always refuse to function at the most important times?

"I've asked Grady to put something in your car," she

went on. "Just to assure you that I really mean what I've said today."

"Thank you, Mrs. Hollinger."

Dazed, I joined Grady in the living room. He suggested that we take a walk. We grabbed our coats and slipped out the back door. As we followed the trail that led into the woods behind the house, the only audible sound was the crackling of leaves underneath our feet.

Grady's hand was warm as he took mine and tucked it into the pocket of his jacket.

"Did Mom talk to you?" he asked as the trees began thickening around us.

"Yeah. I think I'm still in a state of shock."

"She's finally returning to reality. I think she's realized that with or without Neil, the world continues to turn." He stopped and faced me. "I guess it takes some people longer than others, huh?" His dark eyes pierced mine before he put his arm around me and pulled me by his side. When he turned his head to kiss my hair, I felt myself instinctively tense up.

*God, please don't let him feel it.*

But he did.

"What's the matter?" He held me at arm's length. "My kiss isn't good enough for you? Well, don't ever expect it to be different. I'm not after anything, which is more than I could say for Neil."

I gasped and broke away from him. "What do you know about what Neil was after?"

"Forget it. I shouldn't have said that. I'm just so tired of—"

But I wasn't going to forget it. "What makes you think Neil was after anything?"

Grady sighed. "Andrea, Neil never kept his love life a secret. You weren't the first and I'm afraid you wouldn't have been the last."

"But Neil loved me," I said, feeling myself about to break. "I know he did. How could he tell anyone about—"

"Of course Neil loved you. But he wasn't perfect. No more than you and I are perfect. Your relationship with Neil is in the past. I'm not holding anything against you or—"

"I don't believe Neil told you anything," I said coldly, defensively. "You're just assuming."

"What I'm trying to say is that it doesn't make any difference now. It doesn't matter anymore. It's over."

"Oh, but it does matter. It's not over at all. I still love Neil with all my heart, Grady. And if he were still alive, you and I wouldn't be standing here, would we?"

Grady grimaced and turned away from me. "God, I tried, you know I tried." Then he faced me again. "I thought we could make it work, but I can't handle it anymore. I'm sorry."

"I am too. And I don't blame you. I can't handle it anymore myself."

We walked back through the woods in silence. Tears formed in Grady's eyes as I climbed into my car and started the engine.

"I guess I found out about love the hard way," he said so low I had to strain to hear him above the motor. "That must be why I tried so hard . . . because I thought I loved you."

I reached for his hand, but he turned away and walked back up the driveway.

As I drove away, I glanced in my rearview mirror for one more glimpse of him. But the big red teddy bear in the backseat blocked my view.

# 18

$\mathcal{G}$rady had actually said he thought he loved me. In spite of our rocky relationship, at some point in the last few months he'd fallen in love with me.

Had we done the right thing by getting so close to each other? I asked myself that question over and over again as I sat alone in my empty house the remainder of Thanksgiving Day.

We'd given it a fair shot. It was obvious that either I wasn't ready to date yet, or Grady wasn't the right person for me to be involved with. Everything he did or said reminded me of Neil. Under those circumstances, how would I ever get over Neil—even if I wanted to.

That day the clock in the living room seemed to tick louder and move slower than ever before. I expected Grady to call and try to make things right, but he didn't. I'm not sure it would have made any difference, because my intense love for Neil prevented me from caring about Grady or any other guy.

I honestly hadn't meant to hurt Grady. Although breaking off our relationship was probably for the best, I also hurt somewhere deep inside. Maybe I'd allowed Grady a larger part of my heart than I had intended. Why else would I feel this pain?

Possibly the pain I felt was because I'd hurt him. On the other hand, it could be because I'd lost the one person who truly cared about me. If Grady had merely filled a need in my life, then the pain would disappear when I started dating someone else.

But I didn't want to date anyone else.

"God, I'm sorry I hurt him." I began to cry and pray. "I never should've started dating him in the first place."

I stopped abruptly. Was God listening? His presence in my life wasn't as real as it had once been. If God really loved me, then why hadn't He taken away my hurt? Grady told me that the Lord could heal pain. He'd released Grady and Mr. and Mrs. Hollinger from the pain they felt over Neil's death. When was it my turn?

I went to bed early that night. Laying the red teddy bear beside me, I buried my head in its chest and fell asleep.

I skipped church on Sunday because I didn't want to see Grady. I tried to avoid him at school and even succeeded for a while, but our paths finally crossed one day in the hall. I deliberately turned my head when I saw him coming, but he squeezed my arm as we passed each other. When I looked up, he smiled and winked. I'd always appreciated that about Grady. I could depend on him to be himself no matter how difficult the situation seemed to be.

A few days later I found him waiting for me outside of my art class.

"Hi," he greeted.

He'd gotten his hair cut and he was wearing a new shirt.

"That's a nice shirt," I said, biting my lip nervously.

He seemed completely at ease. "Thank you. I missed you at church last week." He looked concerned. "You weren't sick, were you?"

"A little." I couldn't tell him the real reason. I did remember having an upset stomach that day.

As Grady walked me to my next class, he told me about church and basketball tryouts. I had nothing to offer to the conversation. My life seemed to be at a standstill.

I never thought I'd be so happy to see the inside of my

English classroom. I hated English, but walking down the hall with Grady seemed to take forever.

At least now I knew we were still friends. I wasn't so sure that it might not have been easier if we were enemies. I didn't like to admit it, but I missed Grady very much. It might have helped to alleviate my pain if he was mean to me or simply ignored me.

I looked for Grady constantly at school. I was always on guard in case I ran into him, yet at the same time I was scared I wouldn't. My thoughts remained on either Neil or Grady, no matter how hard I tried to think of other things.

Mom was aware that I was no longer dating Grady, but I wasn't willing to open up when she began to press me for details. I didn't want to spoil her happiness by dragging her into my pain.

I stopped going to church and youth meetings. I noticed Cheryl's obvious attempts to flirt with Grady at school, and I didn't feel like watching her do the same at church. I couldn't tell how he felt about her by the way he responded to her. He was always so friendly to everyone.

Neil had been a friendly guy too, but when he decided he didn't like someone, that person knew it.

I dreaded leaving my house because mistletoe, bells, and Santa Claus began to appear everywhere. The whole season seemed to scream out the words: "Christmas is here and Neil isn't!"

Neil had been home most of the month of December the previous year. Being in love with him had made it the very best Christmas I'd ever had.

As much as I missed Neil now, I couldn't help but wonder—what was Grady doing? Who was he buying presents for? Cheryl? Some other girl?

I constantly ached inside and longed for the month of December to end.

One day as I was Christmas shopping downtown I

stopped to stare absently into a store window at a little toy train circling its track. *Reminds me of my life,* I thought dismally—*around in circles with no destination.*

Suddenly Grady, Marc, and Jill approached. "We were just thinking about lunch," Jill remarked. "Why don't you come with us?"

Grady nodded his agreement, probably trying to be polite.

My heart pounded because I stood face-to-face with him. Why should I be so excited to see him? Why did my heart betray me?

As much as I wanted to go, I knew I would have to say no to their invitation for lunch. It would be too awkward for all of us.

"No, but thanks for asking. I'm almost done shopping and I have to be home soon."

Did I read disappointment on Grady's face?

"Are you sure?" Grady's eyes penetrated mine.

"Oh, Marc!" Jill pulled on Marc's arm and pointed to a small gold heart in the window of a jewelry store. "Look at that gold locket. My sister would love it. Let's go in and look at it."

"Okay," Marc agreed. "We'll be back in a minute."

I didn't want to be left alone with Grady. I wanted to run.

"Where have you been?" Grady asked.

"Been?"

"Yeah. I haven't seen you at church or youth meetings or anything. You're not staying away because of me, I hope."

*What an ego,* I thought. *Just like Neil.*

"Why would you think that?"

"Because you never missed church while we were dating. I haven't seen you there since we broke up."

I wished desperately that Marc and Jill would return.

"I—well, I don't exactly have an excuse—it's just that . . ." I suddenly realized I didn't owe Grady Hollinger any explanations. "I've been busy," I said crisply. "How are your parents?"

We made small talk until Marc and Jill emerged from the store.

"We've missed you around church," Jill said.

"I'll try to make it this Sunday," I called over my shoulder as I turned the first corner I came to. I was suddenly tired. That surprise encounter with Grady had drained all my energy. If I didn't truly care about Grady, why was I always so shaken after seeing him?

I'd never felt so lonely. At least after Neil died, I'd had the old crowd to turn to even though they weren't much comfort.

My relationship with my mother had improved tremendously, but now as Chuck became more and more a part of her life, once more the distance between us seemed to be growing.

Chuck seemed more quiet around me. Mom must have told him about my split with Grady. I wondered if she'd also mentioned that I wasn't attending church anymore. He hadn't said anything specific, but I sensed something was wrong. I didn't want Chuck to be disappointed in me.

I didn't want God to be disappointed either. Was God mad at me? What a horrible thought. I decided I would make an effort to get to church that next Sunday. Of course Grady had emphasized many times that going to church didn't make me a Christian, but at least it would start me back in the right direction. I really did want to live for God.

When I awoke on Sunday morning, I felt different. I didn't want to face all those people. I didn't want to see Grady, his parents, or the youth group. Maybe I could hold my own service in my bedroom.

I tried to remember the songs from church. My crackly

voice echoed in the sparsely furnished room, and I visualized God and all His angels covering their ears.

I tried to pray, but I couldn't get past the feeling that I was talking to a stranger—and I knew it wasn't His fault.

Reading the Bible didn't do much for me either. What was wrong? It had been like this ever since Grady and I broke up. Did my relationship with God hinge on my relationship with Grady? I hoped not. Why wasn't I able to reach God?

I tried to pray and read the Bible a few times after that, but the results were the same.

Christmas turned out to be a real bummer. Chuck, Mom, and I exchanged gifts on Christmas Eve, but all I could think about was the beautiful brown leather boots Neil had given me the year before. I remembered our conversation that Christmas Eve night and all the laughs we'd shared. I burst into tears and probably ruined the evening for Chuck and Mom.

I stayed home Christmas Day while Mom visited relatives with Chuck. They'd invited me along, but I didn't want to go.

After watching a boring movie on television, I started to read a book, when the doorbell rang.

The last person I expected on that cold Christmas Day was Grady, yet there he stood on the porch.

I fought the urge to throw myself into his arms and ask him to take me back. I wanted to tell him that I missed him and couldn't live without him, but instead I hardened my feelings and calmly invited him in.

Grady shook his head. "I can't stay. I just stopped by to wish you a Merry Christmas. How are you?"

"I'm fine," I lied.

"I wish I could believe you."

"I'll be okay," I sighed. "It can't hurt forever. Can it?"

"Only if you let it." He paused, giving me a thoughtful

look. "I gave Neil to God. It doesn't bother me so much anymore to think of him because I know where he is and that I'll see him again. That's my hope."

"How can you be so sure?"

"I know God, that's how."

"Well, I know Him too—I think. At this point I'm not sure of anything."

"Andrea, Jesus loves you so much—if you only knew. There's nothing you can do to make Him love you any less."

"Really?"

"Really."

"Thanks. I needed to know that."

There didn't seem to be anything else to say.

"Well, I'll see you around—I hope." Grady began backing down the steps.

"Thanks for coming by."

I closed the door and leaned against it . . . Jesus loved me. He really did. Somehow I had to get my act together, with or without Grady. I would do it only because Jesus loved me.

One night during Christmas vacation I ran into Drew at Smitty's. I'd forgotten about my good intentions and started hanging out there occasionally, hoping to find someone to help me pass the time. I could have easily fallen back into the old crowd. They forever tried to include me in their search for thrills, asking me to drink, party, or hunt for dope.

I wasn't quite that bored—I didn't think.

I was feeling pretty low the night I ran into Drew. He approached the booth where I sat with Nancy, Bruce, and some others.

"Well, look who's here." He smiled when he saw me.

"Hey, Drew, are you going to the New Year's Eve bash at Keller's cabin?" someone asked.

"I wouldn't miss it," Drew returned.

Suddenly everyone was chattering about the upcoming party. Neil had taken me last New Year's Eve. I would never forget it. The party had lasted well into the next day. We'd emptied kegs of beer and danced until our legs felt like Jell-O.

I was a different person then.

Drew was whispering something in my ear.

"I'm sorry, Drew. I didn't hear you."

"I said, why don't you come?" he repeated. "Be my date for the party."

I didn't have a date for New Year's Eve, and it wasn't likely anything would come up. It was only a few days away. Chuck and my mom certainly had plans and wouldn't want to worry about me. I'd managed to handle being lonely so far, but I knew staying home alone on New Year's Eve would send me over the edge.

I needed to be with someone, and it would be fun being with my old friends again.

"Well?" Drew prodded.

"Okay. I'll go."

"You will?" Drew looked surprised. "Wow! I'll pick you up around eight o'clock."

When I decided to go home a few minutes later, Drew walked me out to my car.

"We'll have a great time," he promised.

"I'm looking forward to it."

It was a relief to have something to do on New Year's Eve, and I began to think about the possibilities.

At the same time I wondered what I'd gotten myself into. Maybe I should tell Drew I'd take my own car in case I wanted to leave early.

No, I'd committed myself. This time I would let him decide how long the evening would last.

# 19

When my mother told me about her plans for New Year's Eve, I almost fainted.

"You're going to church?" I repeated incredulously.

"It's not my idea of a good time, but Chuck has been after me to try out your church for a long time. I figured New Year's Eve was as good a time as any. I'm going to start off the new year right for a change."

"Mom, that's great!"

"Actually, at my age, getting drunk on New Year's Eve isn't the big thrill it once was," she admitted. "I'd even like to quit drinking if I can."

"Wow!" I still couldn't quite believe what I was hearing. "I'm really impressed, Mom."

"Well, it's a little too soon for that. I haven't done it yet. You'll be there, won't you?"

"Huh? Be there?"

"At church. I know you haven't been going lately, but you'll be there on New Year's Eve, won't you?"

I couldn't remember when I'd ever felt so rotten or guilty.

"No. I . . . I promised Drew Bradshaw I'd go to a party with him."

"Oh." Mom was plainly disappointed. "Well, you haven't gone on a date with anyone since you and Grady broke up. You deserve it."

I felt awful, really awful. Maybe I could call Drew and

tell him I couldn't make it after all.

Although I was excited about my mother going to church, somehow the idea of spending New Year's Eve there turned me off completely. Grady might be with Cheryl, and the youth group would want to know where I'd been. I wasn't ready to be questioned, nor was I ready to make any kind of commitment to return.

Why should I suffer just because of my mother? She'd go whether I went or not. I'd rather go to the party where I could relax with my old friends.

When Chuck arrived on New Year's Eve, his fuses were already lit and he proceeded to light mine.

Our conversation started off quietly enough.

"Why aren't you going to church?" he asked.

"I have other plans."

"A wild party," Chuck affirmed. "What's the matter with you? That's not like you at all."

"And what is like me?"

"I don't know anymore." He threw up his hands. "You've got me totally confused."

He wasn't the only one who was confused.

"Did you or did you not become a Christian last summer?" he went on.

"I did," I answered meekly.

"Why, you preached more sermons to us during a few short months than I've heard any minister preach in my whole life."

"So?"

"So what happened?"

I didn't know what to say. I felt stupid after all the times I'd preached to him and Mom. Now I would watch them go off to church while I headed for a wild party.

"Oh, Chuck, leave her alone," Mom interjected. "Maybe it's an identity crisis or something."

"Identity crisis," Chuck said cynically.

"I just need to get out—do something different."

"What's different about a wild party?" he asked. "You used to go to them regularly."

I shrugged.

"Well, I am thoroughly disappointed in you," he threw the words over his shoulder as my mother dragged him out the door.

*That makes two of us,* I thought glumly.

I tried to appear cheery when Drew arrived, but it wasn't easy. I climbed into the van and sat close to the door. I'm sure neither one of us knew exactly what to expect from this evening.

"I actually scored another date with you," he remarked as we drove.

"Persistence pays off, I guess," I answered.

"I'm glad I waited it out. I knew you'd get off that religious kick sooner or later."

"It's not a religious kick," I defended. "And just because I'm going to this party doesn't mean I've thrown God overboard."

"Well, this isn't the kind of party religious people go to." Drew chuckled. "Do me a favor and relax tonight. Okay?"

"I'll try."

The party appeared to be well under way when we arrived. It was apparent that some people had already been there all day. Beer bottles, coats, cigarette butts, and bodies were strewn everywhere. The layer of smoke in the air hung so thick I could hardly breathe.

Drew led me through the living room to the kitchen, where a keg sat in the corner. He filled two cups.

"I think I'll pass, Drew," I said.

He stopped pouring and stared at me. "Huh?" Then he smiled. "Oh. You'd rather smoke dope. I've got a couple tabs of acid if you really feel like soaring."

"I think I'll stay straight. I plan to go home sometime tonight."

Drew frowned. "You promised you'd try to relax."

I didn't feel like arguing with him, so I took the cup. I'd pour it out somewhere when he wasn't looking.

I couldn't hide my relief when Rich and Terri entered the kitchen. Somehow I felt safer now.

"What are you doing here?" Terri asked, surprised.

"That's what I just asked myself," I blurted, then glanced sharply at Drew. He was deep in conversation with Rich.

Terri stared at the cup in my hand. "Are you drinking?"

I shook my head and pushed it at her. "Be my guest."

Terri still looked puzzled. "I'm sure surprised to see you here. Especially after last year."

"Last year?"

"Don't you remember this place last year?"

"Vaguely. Neil and I were so stoned—"

"Well, I remember." Terri wrinkled up her face. "I told Rich I didn't want to come near this place tonight, but he wanted to see Drew and some of the other guys from State. We're meeting some people for pizza later and then going to their house where it'll only be a few couples—nice and quiet. She paused and then patted her stomach. "It really makes you mellow out."

A blond girl, obviously drunk, tripped into the kitchen and headed for the keg. She stopped in front of me.

"I remember you," she slurred, waving a finger in my face. "You were here with Neil Hollinger last year. I think I saw you with him at some dances too. Wasn't that sad about his death? I cried for days. He was a sweetie. We dated some last year—the life of the party, wasn't he?"

She was lying. She couldn't have dated Neil. We were going together all through his first year at State.

I glanced at Terri, who immediately turned her head and

tried to pretend she hadn't heard.

"It's nice to see you again." The blonde weaved her way over to the keg.

"She's lying," I told Terri. "She couldn't have dated Neil. We were—"

The look on Terri's face stopped me cold.

"Do you know something, Terri?" I demanded.

She shook her head. "It doesn't matter now, Andrea. Neil's gone."

"Did Neil cheat on me?"

"What difference does it make now?" Terri argued. "Forget it."

"No, I won't forget it. I'd tell you if I ever saw Rich with another girl."

"But Rich is alive," Terri sighed. "What good will it do to drag up stuff about Neil now? Don't you want to remember the good things?"

"I do, but I'm nobody's fool. If he was playing around, I have a right to know."

"It's no big deal. Rich and I drove down to see Neil one weekend and he took her out. That's all. It was nothing, really."

"Nothing?" I screeched. "Neil lied to me. He told me he never took anyone else out." Rich and Drew looked over at us and I lowered my voice. They resumed their conversation. "How could he do that if he really loved me?" I hissed.

"Don't feel so bad about it," Terri spoke gently. "All college guys do it. They get bored. Neil did love you, though."

"I got bored too, but it never occurred to me to date anyone else."

"Guys are different."

"Yeah, but he lied to me. . . ."

Drew moved to my side then, grinning. "You two can chitchat anytime." He pulled on my arm. "C'mon. Let's go someplace where we can get better acquainted."

I didn't want to get better acquainted. What I wanted was to go home. My evening had been ruined. Neil had cheated on me—he'd even lied about it. I remembered my conversation with Grady about Neil using harder drugs. I'd refused to believe it. Now I wondered if Grady had been telling the truth.

I supposed it was a prime example of blind love. In my eyes Neil could do no wrong. Dead or alive, he was the epitome of perfection to me.

I didn't want to think about him being any less than I remembered him to be—my infallible leader and lover. "Let's go down to the basement," Drew suggested. "It's usually quieter down there."

It seemed awfully noisy all right. The beat of the stereo shook the whole house and everyone screamed at one another, trying to be heard above it.

As we neared the stairs, Drew released my arm.

"Wait here. I need to talk to someone."

He disappeared into the next room. I waited, but a minute turned into five. I decided to move around a little.

A few couples danced wildly in the living room. Everywhere I looked couples were making out, oblivious to their surroundings.

The marijuana smoke began to make me lightheaded, so I decided to go outside for some fresh air. I bumped into Nancy and Bruce on the porch.

"Look, Bruce, she's really here just like Drew said she would be!" Nancy cried. "Are you finally done with that religious stuff?"

"No, I just—"

"Isn't this quite a bash?" she cut in. "We've been here all day. Around midnight things will really get hopping." She grabbed Bruce's arm. "C'mon. I'm dying for a beer. See ya later, Andrea."

A bash? Apparently everyone in there thought this was

living it up. They'd never known anything else. This was their escape from reality.

I knew many of the kids. They lived from thrill to thrill. In between thrills their problems threatened to overcome them. They had no idea how to deal with peer pressure and the confusion and hurt of their broken homes. How could I ever have thought I'd be able to fit in with these people tonight? I'd never felt so uncomfortable in all my life. Something had really happened to me that night at the Dayspring concert. I'd met God and I'd never be the same again.

With or without Neil, with or without Grady, I wanted to stay a Christian. Although I missed Neil terribly, I'd always felt an underlying peace and joy when I thought about the reality of God's presence in my life. In the last few weeks since I had pushed God away, I felt empty inside.

*God, please forgive me,* I cried softly. *I want to be as close to you as I was last summer.*

The door flew open behind me and I turned to see Drew scowling at me.

"I asked you to wait right there," he frowned. "I've been looking all over for you."

"I'm sorry," I apologized. "I needed some fresh air."

*God, help me through this night.* Drew would be furious if I asked him to take me home.

Drew downed a bottle of beer and leered at me. "That's okay. I was just a little worried. You need to stick with me. There're all kinds of jerks around here who prey on innocent girls."

He took my hand and I followed him downstairs where it was quiet and dark. I could see shadows and knew we weren't alone, but that wasn't much of a comfort.

"I remember there being a Ping-Pong table down here," I told Drew. "How about a game?"

Drew chuckled. "Very funny."

As my eyes grew accustomed to the dim lighting in the

basement, I saw that we had entered a little room. Suddenly Drew pushed me down on what felt like a bed. I tried to pull away, but his grip tightened.

"Drew, let go. You're hurting my arm."

He loosened his hold but didn't release me.

"C'mon, we're done playing your game. Let's play mine for a change. Don't play Miss Goody-Goody—Neil told me about you. I've been waiting for this for a long time."

"What do you mean Neil told you about me?" I demanded.

"You want me to spell it out? We were fraternity brothers and roommates. What do you think we talked about, the weather? He told me about all of them."

I gulped. "All of them?" Shock turned into disbelief.

"I know you wanted to believe that you were Neil's only love. I just spoiled it for you. Sorry." And then his lips were on mine, hard and demanding.

With all my strength I kicked him in the leg. He let out a yelp and let go of my arm. In one leap, I crossed the room. As I fumbled for the door, I felt his hands on my shoulders, jerking me around.

"Leave me alone!" I cried. "I just want to go home."

"Look, sweetheart. Nobody forced you to come to this party. It's a long drive up here. If you want to go home, feel free. I'm staying. And don't worry about me bothering you anymore! I've had it with you! No girl is worth all this!"

He stalked out angrily and left me alone.

*God, thank you,* I whispered. I couldn't remember when I'd been so scared.

What now? Was I doomed to stay at this crazy party all night?

# 20

*M*y mind raced as I fumbled my way across the dark basement to the stairs. My mother wasn't home, and I was sure it was useless to call the church office. No one would answer. Who else could I call?

Then I remembered Rich and Terri. *Oh, God, please let them still be here,* I whispered. Terri had sounded anxious to leave.

During the time Drew and I had been in the basement, more people had crammed into the cabin. I frantically searched faces as I moved among the crowd. I became more and more frightened. How would I find them with all these people around? What if I ran into Drew again?

At last I saw them standing by the back door talking to two guys. I almost threw myself into Terri's arms with relief.

Terri's eyes widened when she saw me. "Are you okay, Andrea?"

"Yeah—sure. Uh—can I get a ride home with you?"

"Of course. We were just leaving now. What about Drew?"

"Please don't ask. I don't want to talk about him."

Fortunately, Rich and Terri didn't press the issue. We began the long drive back into town.

"Wild party, huh?" Rich remarked.

"Too wild for me," I answered. A sudden thought occurred to me. "Would you drop me off at my church?"

I didn't want to go home to an empty house. It was only

ten-thirty, and I knew the service would last until after midnight.

"You have a church service tonight?" Rich sounded interested. "That's what you Christians do on New Year's Eve?"

"I don't think it's so much a celebration of New Year's Eve as it is an excuse to get together. Christians enjoy being together." I hesitated. "Would you like to come in for a minute?"

"We've got to meet somebody," Rich returned. "But we might drop by someday in the near future. Terri and I have been talking a lot about God recently. We've realized just how much we don't know."

"I think I'd be a basket case right now if it wasn't for God," I admitted.

"Neil's death hit you the hardest," Terri sympathized. "We all know that."

"Yeah. But I think I'll be okay now."

"I never doubted that," Terri said as we pulled up in front of the church.

"Well, I sure did. Thanks for the ride. You'll never know how much I appreciate this."

After they drove away, I stood on the sidewalk staring at the church. It was brightly lit up, warm and inviting. It was quite a contrast to the dark party I'd just escaped from. I was glad I could leave the shadows in the past.

Did I want to leave Neil in the shadows? I suddenly realized that I wasn't leaving him in the shadows at all. I believed heaven was now Neil's home. That was all I needed to know.

It felt good to be back. As I neared the door, I heard singing. It sounded loud and exciting. I slipped quietly into a back pew. The church was full, but I immediately spotted my mother and Chuck a few rows in front of me. I couldn't see Grady.

The congregation sang two more songs and then Pastor Thorsen announced that we'd take a break for fellowship and sandwiches in the basement.

I hurried down the aisle to meet Mom and Chuck. When they saw me, a look of surprise and joy passed over their faces.

"Well, what brings you here tonight?" Chuck asked. "The party get boring?"

"Not exactly boring," I hedged. "Just not my speed."

He smiled sheepishly. "I apologize for my attitude earlier this evening. I had no right to try to manipulate you."

"I should have listened to you," I said, staring at the floor.

As we followed the crowd downstairs, Chuck put his arm around me and squeezed my shoulders.

"How do you like my church, Mom?"

"It's very nice. The people seem friendly. They certainly are excited about their faith."

"That's what I like about it," Chuck put in. "These people are alive."

"It helps me to understand why you've wanted to spend so much time here," Mom admitted. Then she added thoughtfully, "You know, by being here tonight, a lot of things are becoming clear."

"Like what?"

"Oh, just some things. I'm not quite ready to discuss them yet."

She had become interested in spiritual things lately, and I was sure it was just a matter of time until she asked Christ into her life. It would take a conscious effort on my part not to push her.

As we talked, I kept an eye out for Grady. Once downstairs, we made our way to the refreshment table. A couple of girls from the youth group approached saying they were glad to see me. I began to believe it when others continued to greet me.

"Look who's here. I've really missed you."

"It's great to see you. Where have you been?"

"I've called you lots of times, but you're never home."

I really did have a place in the lives of this group, a place where I belonged.

But where was Grady?

Marc and Jill were the next friendly faces I saw.

"Andrea!" Jill squealed. "It's so good to see you."

"Yeah," Marc agreed. "We thought you'd forgotten all about us."

"Not at all. I could never forget about you."

"Just because you and Grady aren't dating anymore doesn't mean you have to drop all of us," Jill teased.

"Uh—where is he anyway?" I tried to sound casual.

"Who?"

"Grady. Is he here tonight?"

Jill looked puzzled. "Yeah, I saw him. He's here—somewhere."

"I think he said something about going to make more punch," Marc said. "There are a lot more people here than we expected."

It was just like Grady to be helping out.

Marc and Jill moved on. A moment later I saw Grady come through the kitchen door carrying a bowl filled with fruit punch. As eager as I was to talk to him, I suddenly felt shy. Maybe he wouldn't want to talk to me. Maybe he was with Cheryl tonight.

Suddenly from out of nowhere she appeared, looking as pretty as ever. She began helping him fill the cups with punch.

Soon the fellowship time would be over and I'd miss the opportunity to talk to him.

I didn't deserve Grady Hollinger. He'd been so good to

me and I'd treated him like a possession to be used whenever I felt like it. I'd played with his feelings and caused him nothing but hurt. It would serve me right if he never spoke to me again.

What if I had ruined any possibility of our ever having a close relationship? Maybe it was too late to try again. I began to realize that it wasn't so much what we wanted for ourselves that mattered but what God wanted for us. Did He want us together? I had to find out.

I watched Cheryl chatter away as they filled cup after cup.

Grady wasn't paying much attention to her. However, he didn't look unhappy, just preoccupied.

*God, please let him stop filling those cups and look up,* I prayed. *Let him see me before it's time to go upstairs. I can't make the first move because I'm not sure how he feels about me.*

It wasn't long before Grady lifted his head. When our eyes met from across the room, I felt as if ten bolts of lightning had struck. I was surprised everyone in the room didn't notice.

Grady unknowingly was pouring punch all over the table, and Cheryl was frantically mopping it up, trying to get his attention. I couldn't help giggling at the funny sight. The spell broke when Grady realized what he'd done. He tried to mop the wet tablecloth with a towel and then left Cheryl as he hurried across the room to where I stood.

"You came," he spoke softly. He took my hand and twined his fingers through mine. It felt so good to stand there facing Grady, our hands locked together. Everyone seemed to fade out of my realm of vision, and I felt as if Grady and I were the only people in the whole world.

"Grady, I need to talk to you." I looked around the room. Almost all the people had left.

"Sure. We'll just wait until everyone goes upstairs and then go sit over there by the fire. Okay?"

Chuck promised to save me a seat. I watched my mother and him as they headed back upstairs.

"I was sure surprised to see them here," Grady said.

"Yeah," I agreed.

When the room was finally empty, Grady went to turn off some of the lights, and then we went and sat by the soft glow from the fire. As I sat on the hearth and watched him try to get the dying flames to blaze, I began to see the many qualities I admired in him: his gentleness, his sensitivity to others, his seriousness. These were not the qualities I'd enjoyed in Neil.

Neil and I had many good times together. We'd laughed, joked, teased. But I suddenly realized how little we had talked to each other. Neil had been a clown, and we all expected it of him and loved him for it. Grady was more intense and I appreciated that. Neil could not be depended upon, yet I had never seen that as a fault. I had learned to expect it. Grady was totally dependable. I loved that about him. They may have been alike in some ways, but their unique and special qualities had affected my life in two different ways.

Did I love Grady? Possibly love was a process, something one grew into. If that was true, I was surely falling in love with Grady Hollinger—for who he was.

I felt extremely shy again. What if I told him how I honestly felt and he didn't respond? Maybe he didn't care anymore.

When the fire was once again roaring, he sat down on the hearth beside me. Neither of us spoke for a moment. We watched the fire, stealing occasional glances at each other.

"It feels right, doesn't it?" Grady spoke first. "Our being here together, I mean."

That was all the encouragement I needed.

"It does. Grady, I've missed you."

"I've missed you too." His eyes held mine. "Where have you been?"

"I've been nowhere and back." I studied the toes of my shoes. "Yet God still loves me, like you told me at Christmas."

"Where's—where's Neil?"

I sensed how much it hurt him to have to ask.

"In heaven, where he belongs. I guess now I can be where I belong."

"Where do you belong, Andrea?"

"Grady, will you hold me?"

His eyes searched mine. "Are—are you sure? I've been restraining myself for the last fifteen minutes," he said.

"I'm sure."

He pulled me into a close embrace that seemed to melt away all my uncertainties. We held each other for a long time. Then in the distance we heard the exploding of firecrackers and the ringing of church bells. Voices were wishing each other a Happy New Year. A new year which, for me, marked a new beginning.

"It's been a long night, hasn't it?" Grady whispered.

"It sure has," I answered softly. "But I think the morning is finally here."